T0164335

THE KAFKA CHRONICLES

THE KAFKA CHRONICLES

MARK AMERIKA

BLACK ICE
BOOKS

Published by FC2 with support given by the English Department Unit for Contemporary Literature of Illinois State University and the Illinois Arts Council

Address all inquiries to: FC2, Unit for Contemporary Literature, Campus Box 4241, Illinois State University, Normal, IL 61790-4241.

The Kafka Chronicles
Mark Amerika

ISBN: Paper, 0-932511-54-6

Produced and printed in the United States of America

Cover image: Jean C. Lee

For Fran

CONTENTS

VILLAGE TRIPPING

niceties niceties   nice cities   (don't exist)   meanstreets
                                                      meanstreaks
                                                      means&ways

falling headfirst into the pavement our buoy of boys
    cracks his numskull and turns more nonsensical
derivation   inside/out & backwards   (summer
salt   wintry peppering)

Tuesday was okay   Thursday he had a plan   Friday
  he was out roaming the meancitystreets   Saturday
he slept late   Sunday he wrote a little   Monday he
woke up feeling like blowing it all away   Monday
night's marginalia took him over   soon he was
Tuesday morning looking for a new gig   the plan
had decentered   too bad for our buoy of boys   his
  nuclear family holocaust was hollow and cost a
bundle to repair   the damage was irreparable or so it
turned out   so he began shooting stars with
speed   pretty soon he had a gig as bagman for a
CBGB shitband everything was going supergroovy
I thought I saw him dead on Astor Place but that
was some space chick from Missouri   Amber was

her name   she had been dumped near the great
cube   the rolling spinning turning statuesque
personification of a geometric gentrified neighborly
 transmogrification   her heart was stone   her mind
was stoned   Lois E. Sider and her kid sis Apple Sider
say that Amber used to whore around Saint Mark's
Church   it's really too much   I'm gonna forget
it   Saint Marx was a bad man or so I hear them
calling

brain fried and scrambled maybe sunny side up
sweet disposition   honey can you take out the
garbage   so I go for a walk   where to take this shit
(I wonder) if only words could recycle   Too late for
a bold cure   gotta face reality   The Ecocycle Truck
rides by I start chasing it Here   take this   I throw
myself into the truck it turns me into blueprint

now I'm feeling architectonic   I go to a bar   The
Grass Roots   drink a tonic   grease my hair with yet
still more tonic   all I need now is a relatively mild
form of detoxification   I can hear them calling me
by name   Saint Marx they yell   I'm not a Marx   I
yell back   *I'm an animal*   well Mark   the truth
comes out   Saturday creeps into the bedroom like a
nun in a bikini asking me where do I find Saint
Charles Place   I say New Orleans   you can't miss
 it   all the parades go down it on Mardi Gras   the
trolley rides up and down it   you can't miss it   but
I *do* miss it   and now it's late March   one month

too late   never enough Sundays   Friday was the
beginning of the workweek   I wrote a nuclear
education piece called "Unclear"   Saturday I took
off for a little eco ramification principal player in the
ensuing garbage scene was Me   plus Apple Sider
and oh yeah a cameo by our buoy of boys   what's
his name   I forget   doesn't matter   fact is he slept
late   overslept   yes   so very much unlike him
usually the kind to get up on time   eat a good
breakfast   make it to the workspace   start honking
on the tele   tele-ing everybody that he's alive and
well and doing the dirty deed and dog eat dogging
and do or dying and driving The Big One home
jeez I can't wait for Wednesday

Alkaloid Boy meets The End Is Nearing and reevaluates his
current position. Flinging out long scroll he goes over the
balance sheet mesmerized with its condition. Movement
ratio untouched unencumbered transient feedback loop
outside the vicious circle no hawks to ward off no chastity
belt to slow him down. Meanwhile the growing Big Death
hid away inside The Death Terminal's central location
computer virus spreading facts sheet distorted "just when
you thought you had your program under control you find
out that it has a mind of its own." Somewhere in the neutral
column lay Blue Sky. She's more than the indian selfadhesive
facility that keeps your body broken in and mind mattered.
She's the loose canon free whistle love hassle-free blowjob
nuke warm tomb mama womb mama. It all spreads out

everlasting hope peace love care. You can see it in her face. The way she does her hair.

Ancient rock star from other planetary consciousness in a time still not known to Man. Alkaloid Boy growing into the rough discursive passages of The Black Death and its Terminal Blues perception. No gloom and doom here boys. Just blatant disregard for mutual laughter easygoing pyrotechnics love's alabaster wings serenade symposium. None of it. The upper of the Upper feigning heroics getting rich. The lower of the Upper poorly performing cheap imitations of their hierarchical master geniuses. Then the vast middle of Everybody losing it slowly wondering how in the hell slave labor technology turned into the heavy burden. Many clothes draping the monster new technology. Many fashions dining the plates of the masters. Many new plates of pictures shining on the dead reel of the Platonic masters. The genius overload fortified to kill. Blue Sky looking into the Big Sky seeing The Black Death hovering spiritually resounding throughout the heavens Her motor desiring The End Is Nearing while Alkaloid Boy tries to make a comeback. Music videos show the old man balding. His voice whispers soundtrack backlash: "alkaloid boy / he's very nervous / alkaloid boy / you can see it in his delivery…"

You're here for Youth. Youth is eternal until The Black Death does its final number. Until then it's Youth. Either that or die a slow death of usury. Use. Use and re:use. Re;use and re/fuse. Isometric exercises compounded by daily withdrawal into isotopic future's realignment clause. Why? Because because

because because. Because The Death Terminal's central bank location has videotape information leading to the facts. Never mind the computer virus slow death takeover. Never mind the terrorist indoctrination full liability comprehensive plan. Never mind the collection agency's pedantic perusal of your bodily flesh. Excise your sin taxes and levy the poisoned language juice in their artless direction. Turn strong social impacts into natural make-up compacts and see how they run like peegs from a numb see how they fly.

Blue Sky calls me over the intercom to say she's all lost in the secret agent boiling bubbling hot love lava of last night. Easy happy going coming. Super stroll in the autumn bowl. Leaves of her ass strumming electric blue guitar notes against my despotic numbed musculature. Freedom tongues rolling hot saliva sweat over the creamy dew drop madness moisture. Heaven and Earth. Wild lustful forestry energy. Trees on the horizon in a natural burn. The moral equivalent of our founding fathers. Eating clear Blue Sky heaven juices cleansing insides reeling years morning dreams thundered pleasure lightning happiness eyes wide open. Summer shower tar pits kneel. The feel of plunder.

More Black Death resounding throughout the skies above little twitches in the face responding humanly despondent responding. "I'm gonna run for The House change some things turn back the clock to Eden..." : easy going open heart mind electric blue sky numb hope peace care flesh free

BLAST!!
BLAST!!!!!!!!!!!!!!!!!!!!!!BLAST!!!!!!!!!!!!!!!!!!!!!!!!!!!!!!!!!BLAST!!!!!!!!!!!!!!!!!!!!!!!!!!!!!!!!!
the lower of the lower of the lower of the lower of the lower
of the lover of the loner of the lower of the loner of the lover
of the   B !!   L !!!   A !!   S !!!   T !!

The shack shakes and rattles. Smacks of independence(?).
The shits are coming!! The shits are coming!! Before we can
put on our excess clothing drapery refinements fashionable
chic motif in a new wave nightclub pretentiously portraying
the scene of our lifeless generation the feds bust in ::: Bureau
Chiefs (says The Big Wig). Are you Alkaloid Boy?

I was Alkaloid Boy until you guys gentrified the world. Now
I'm occasionally employed by the Jacksonville Public Library. Dealing with the indigents. Our growing traffic problems are a direct tribute to you and your oft spoken of leader
The Great Producer. Is he still alive?

Never you mind Alkaloid Boy you're under arrest. Who's the
babe?

I'm no babe you pig shithead I'm Blue Sky and I represent this
too harassed heavy metal genius of other-worldly consciousness.

No such thing as an other-worldy consciousness sweety
better get yer facts straight (she looks at him / her face is
swollen and full of my cummmm). We got it all on the fact
sheets. Spread dead and ready to go. We can put out your
story faster than you can dream up a new name sister. Hey.

Wait a minute. Don't I know you? Weren't you Sister Slew in that ear droning nightmare demonstration we bombarded back in 92?

Look pig shithead you may be The Great Producer's loyal Bureau Chief but that doesn't dismiss the fact that my client and I have our god given rights as unalienated beings doing our own thing here in...

Fuck the facts sweety you've got two minutes to get your shit together or we're taking you as you are. Okay boys. Start burning...

Symbiotic conflagrations burning persisting desiring the mode made contagious and spreading all over the facts sheet balance sheet clean reading sheets slowly preambling a long and ever needed silence. Yours is Youth I can hear a voice whisper to me. Yours is to make up the despondent truce and then break out free swinging reluctant renegade. Keep the fires burning. Toil in the making and give for the taking. Rake in the mind some extra sensitive leaves of flesh and intermesh with the golden locks of the linked Blue Lady. Terminal dysfunctional regional start-up. Slow expansion of the peripheral phases on the edges moving in. Satellite superstardom promiscuous selling of the idea in the form of fleshy things!! What perfect timing!! Just as the tyrants finally got hold of something real and useable the switches blew and the hub hastened progress. More storms later. Many more. Writing's sweet revenge on the numb. The num is out there

                    1 or 0
                    afford
                    o lord
                    ignore
                    abhor

arbor equals tree.
it's official.
The troops are climbing high in pinstripes army stripes marines.
The upper of the Upper.
resounding in the heavens.
Blue Sky laughs eye dying
piercing stinging madness.
civilization

at a standstill

standing

             falling

standing

             falling

standing

             falling

still

     still

             life

Decharacterization: first and foremost / high on the list of things

To Do

1) evil eyed optimist
2) puritanical pessimist
3) retrograde renegade
4) easygoing numskull
5) taxing interest
6) megalomaniacal monsterman
7) persevering wanderer
8) sunshiny souvenir
9) sovereign veneer
10) venereal vegetarian
11) pornosophic filmmaker
12) college student
13) bank president
14) beatnik historian
15) girl watcher
16) punky playboy
17) diseased dyslexic
18) monkey grammarian
19) existentialist outlaw
20) linguistic statesman
21) early riser
22) effervescent eunuch
23) egghead eavesdropper
24) neoconservative butcher
25) egotistical holyman
27) continue the discontinue

28)   still crazy after all these years
29)   butcher the butcher
30)   wearisome whacker
31)   where art thou waterfall?
32)   butcher the butcher
333)   dead meat   dead meat   dead meat   dead meat
421)   off to the boonies
5X1r#217)   name   address   social   security   perforation
dis
int
egr
ati
on!

final mishapover
 B L O W N
pro ./ por ./ tions

eros intensification

Alkaloid Boy and Blue Sky meet up with another couple who go by the names Hair Monster and Rose Hips. Hair Monster looks kind of like the protagonist in the film ERASERHEAD although his persona and presence remind you more of Sergy Eisenstein. His light eyes shine in the dark and you'll often feel the weight of his prolonged silences as they surround and eventually control the action being generated in the scene you share with him. Rose Hips is a She-Ra love goddess who has something for everyone. Her energy adds to Hair Monster's energy and together the fields of force go whacko. You get the feeling you're going out on your first eco-anarcho double date. There's no Weatherman-like bomb-exploding going to go on here, no Black Panther rabble-rousing. Just energy shock waves sending electric love currents all throughout the mise en scène. A major motion picture. A creature feature starring friction and static with a cameo by mystical genius.

Alkaloid Boy is telling Hair Monster about the unexpected wake-up call he and Blue Sky received from The Bureau Chiefs.

"They were lost in the mid-twentieth century, man, I mean you wouldn't believe it. They had it all covered in one major crackup: breaking and entering, illegal search and seizure, unwarranted arrests and, of course..."

Hair Monster raised his index finger to his lips and said Shhh.

Rose Hips made an expression like I know, we've already been there.

Blue Sky whispered that she thought the page was being bugged.

Big Artist Man appeared out of nowhere and said Hey, watch out, they'll throw you in the pit for resisting slave labor technocratic nightmare.

Isreal Disreal threw up his hands in passive disgust and said Win some Lose most.

M/F an old friend recently taken out of the pit and put back on the contaminated soil said Don't kvetch it's worse down there.

Willa Thrilla sold out. She's buying tutti-fruity gunshot for the kids at war.

New Anima is now Nude Arsenal. S/he is busy inventing a religion that wipes out supply/demand via autosuck restitution full money back guarantee.

Open your eyes and tell me what you see.

HANGING OUT
AT THE CAFE SAVOY

Sin Handling was overloading on wicked thoughts that made her feel totally uncomfortable around him.

He had just met her at the Cafe Savoy drinking ginseng tea reading another spy-sex novel by Karel Atwood. Atwood was a local author who frequented the Savoy.

Somebody would be speeding and nervous enough to approach her and then the deal would be cut. The revolution would be televised after all. Sin was handling this energy better than expected.

She was comfortable with him. She was a cafe reading ginseng tea and then the deal. A local author who was handling this spy-sex novel better than expected, was overloading. Somebody would spread the newsprint on her swollen belly and the revolution would smear.

Tortuous music encapsulated the nightmare technocracy in just under four minutes. Her beauty marks were commercial breaks subliminally forecasting the facsimile of nature's imminent death. Squads of mod godheads sipping espresso dreamt about the program's takeover. Overloading on him, naked in a spy-sex novel, she spread a tortuous revolution on his chest in just under four minutes. Sin was handling this better than drinking ginseng tea.

The facsimile of nightmare technocracy dreamt about the godhead nervous enough to approach her and be televised after all. This energy would smear the local author and then the deal would be cut. Encapsulated commercial. Breaks forecasting imminent death squads losing integrity as they come closer together. Freer in densely populated counterinsurgencies that made her feel totally uncomfortable. Nervous enough to deal.

Somebody would smear. A local author. The revolution was handling this better than sin. Beauty marks on her belly encapsulated the spy-sex novel. Karel was comfortable with her. An added touch of wickedness. Nobody but you subliminally forecasting the dream of revolution televised by the local author at the Cafe Savoy where Sin was approaching Karel after all.

He offered her his hand in marriage. She said he was too encapsulated. Their fingers peeled off until only the bone mattered. Drinking ginseng tea they read the newsprint. Dreamt about the nightmare. The program's takeover with an added touch of integrity. They come closer together. Better than expected.

IRIS

1

come to think of it   it all started when i went to visit my
mother who at the time was living fifteen minutes from
miami beach   i had just returned from a completely made-
up lifestory in europe where everything i wrote in new york
the months previous to my departure started happening
with very little variation   now in north miami   the place
where they assure me i was born (i'm still not convinced
seeing how young i was then i can't even begin to remember)   i was bored to death with nothing to do except plan a
possible trip to mexico   a chance to spend some of the
money i made as a freelance bicycle courier in new york city
the summer of the year in question (always in question   time
having lost all relevance long ago)   with mother working
her brains out (literally out   see it all the time   family and
friends with so much performance potential losing it all to
the routine of giving up their SELF to the greedy needs of the
MULTI-NATIONAL BLACK HOLES & THEIR DOPED-UP
STOOGES)   i had finally bought a ticket with air mexicana
and had about ten days to kill in sunny florida so i decided
to do the only thing there was to do (was it a conscious
decision on my part or was i forced to go with what was
available at the time thus limiting my freedom completely
and making me nothing but a small stooge who only dreamt

of rambunctious recklessness?) i went to the beach carrying my bongos and knapsack full of fruit and trail mix plus a small bag of weed i stole from my mother's top drawer (i remember her telling me before she went off to work that she would prefer it if i didn't take any of her pot, not that she smokes it anymore, she doesn't, but she all of a sudden felt that it wasn't such a great idea for a mom to turn her visiting son on to the evils of stoned madness, you know what it's like, Just Say No, who could say Yes, what would they be if they actually outgrew the need to become part of the moral monopoly and said something positive like YES I'M INTO SMOKING A LITTLE WEED EVERY NOW AND THEN IT RE-LEAVES ME OF BRUTAL SOCIETAL TENSIONS i took her remarks as an invitation and copped the whole bag or what was left of it and brought it to the beach) my first footsteps on the sand were accompanied by the smell of the sea salt air and the voice of some foreign woman who said quite simply "bon jour" and as i looked up i saw a rather attractive middle-aged woman in a blue one-piece with a big straw hat on her head that she held down with one hand so that the strong breeze that blew off the ocean wouldn't blow it off her head (i remember the first thing i felt when i heard this woman's french accent was something like DESIRE an anonymous master guitarist picking a hardcore rock solo in the pit of my being something that forces itself on you a kind of internal recognition whereby you recognize this other person inside of you whose occasional appearances here and there remind you that there's definitely something out there to play around with sometimes i think this other person is FATE at other times i figure it's just ME the real ME the one i never really have enough time for but am constantly in search of finding once again so that i might turn on the love mechanism whose sole objective is to transgress the power blockage that precludes my pleasure-bearing self from becoming the one thing it needs to become over and over again   WOMAN   this becoming-WOMAN consciousness that collects like highly concentrated resin inside the tube of an overused bong is always seeping out of me at just the right time   feeling nothing now but the fuel-injected DESIRE ITSELF   being nothing but THAT   now going after something i have no idea what it is or even if it's really there but the possibility entices me to the point of rapid increase in circulation building stockpile of saliva hidden turmoil milkshaking my blender balls

ready to immediately respond to this woman with the hat about to fall off her head)   "bon jour" is my reply to her and since i speak her language she stops her lateral movement about ten yards in front of me and says "parlais vous francaise?" in which case i don't but tell her in my best amerikan idiom that my recent exploits in europe afforded me the opportunity to render delicious the sound of a french woman when she spoke to anyone anywhere within my listening proximity   i don't believe she was interested in all of that but she did come closer and grab my arm and asked me to come for a walk   it was only then that i realized that she wasn't middle-aged at all (although she sure did have the body of a forty year old) but rather she was a much older woman   perhaps mid-sixties at youngest   beautiful face that must have been surgically altered   grey eyes that spoke death in whispers of co-conspiracy as if she were tel-ling me something like "i know you know...now i want you to just forget about it and play along with me..." which i obeyed because for me   whenever a woman of the world (which she was   it was obvious from the start) aggressively permits herself to take control of me then that's exactly what i let her do   it's one of my many roles   i call it THE INVISIBLE MAN   it's like i'm there but i'm not there   i smell like a human fucking another human but i'm not there   i breathe heavy and grunt like an animal fucking another animal but i'm not there   I'M INVISIBLE   it's my favorite role   i just sit back and let the imagination roll

yes   i give credit to the imagination only   not HER   not ME   just collective imagination   fictional energy presenting itself as nothing but form   form forming nothing but form itself   many times taking on the shape of some of the wildest strangest sexual experimentation the human flesh has ever had the chance to experience

we walked for about a mile and then she pointed out her beach towel and umbrella and that's where we parked ourselves for the next half hour or so (she immediately began touching me all over   especially as i started playing the moroccan bongos i bought the weekend before in disney's epcot center what i was doing at disney i'll leave you to figure out   the music seemed to stir something up inside her   my approach to the whole scene was serene yet concerted in my attempts to derive a superhip sex vibe from the skins as if the playing itself could somehow do my seducing   it had before   why not now?   the more i played the more i realized she was getting turned on to me   twenty minutes into the playing she had her hand on my thigh right near my hardening cock which was very respondent to the idea of handjob or gumjob or buttfuck or anything this ageless whisper of death had to offer it   the heat emanating from my erection was sending an advisory warning to the lips of

death itself   i was projecting my future onto her)   "take me
back to your place"   "i'm old enough to be your
mother"   "no, you're old enough to be my grandmother
but that doesn't matter baby cuz you're so alive with the
beauty of your experience and besides your hand has got me
playing like i never played before"   everything i said to her
was true   her hands   it ends up   were the things that
turned me on most   there's always something that does
it   many times it's not even physically measurable   it's just
a look   or a phrase   a situation   but here it was a combina-
tion of all these things with the Capitol of Turn On being the
palms of her hands   and she knew this   i don't know how
she knew this   she just intuited my DESIRE unfolding in her
hands as they massaged my thighs and waist and soon my
neck and i may be wrong but for some reason my memory
is saying that as soon as she commented on her being old
enough to be my mother and me immediately saying grandmother it was right then that she took a quick snap at my
cock bulging inside my bathing suit   i was seriously losing
my head trying to figure out how NOT to maneuver myself
on top of her right there on the beach   place my cock into
the grey matter of her WANTED DEAD OR ALIVE pussy   the
thing she was keeping at a distance from me always using her
hands to shape my body which was nothing but clay desire
ready to be molded by the next femme fatale that would take
a chance with me   here in the age of NO CHANCE   where
to have access is to just be around it all as it teases and teases
and teases you until finally it squeezes all the love out of you
and you have NO CHOICE IN THE MATTER   the choice
having already been made for you thanks to LIMITED
FREEDOM PERSONIFIED BY THE MANUFACTURING OF
CONSENT   so all you end up doing is copping out a position

in the organizational superstructure's hierarchical bureaucracy trying to out-manipulate the next guy who wants to see
you MELT ON THE SCENE

but i wasn't thinking these things five years ago when in the
presence of IRIS (that was my matron of the arts' now
notorious name)   IRIS had my pupils dilated   i was trip-
ping on her unconditional love of play   she turned the
whites of my eyes into poached eggs which she would
serve   happily serve   with whole wheat toast and french
roast coffee   a special blend she brought down to miami
beach with her every winter so that she could still have a taste
of home during her sojourn (before it gets too confusing i
should say that her home was not france but quebec
city   yes   my warm melting mama was a quebeçois queen
who was surely dying of cancer and wanted to have one last
stab at sexual fulfillment before she would go   and i would
go with her too   whether she liked it or not   i would have
to go with her)

2

A terrible sadness resonates throughout my body as I write of Iris, the sixtysomething melting mama of gumjob fame and definite fortune (accumulated over the years). That first gumjob with its Deep Throat customariness made me feel like I had conquered the whole fucking world. Ego boost? Not really (although who's to say?). More like an energetic mind boost that made going home to visit mom a very interesting experience. Mom would ask "Where have you been today? You look so handsome." (She was genuinely surprised at how good I could look when I dressed up nicely.) "Oh, I just went to the beach. Walked around." When in actuality I had found myself walking the park with Iris. Our foreplay (just writing about it now, some five years later, sends the same Invisible Man [Fate?] running around inside my entire body...why does he always end up in the same place? My nuts are stirring with passion...if she hadn't died on me I'd still be her young not-so-dumb full-of-cum MTV rockstar ramming and jamming electric heavy metal riffs up into her endless insatiable pit of narcissism and need)...our foreplay consisted in me calling her up on the phone and arranging a meeting at the JFK Memorial Torch where the first thing we did was kiss (deep french, everything goes) and then without a moment passing immediately held hands and started to walk. I've already mentioned her hands. Just

like the lycra and gyrating hips on MTV hypnotize a generation of would-be consumers   Iris' hands did something to
me that made this shit-life worth all the effort. Thirty
minutes of walking the park holding on to my I-ree-I's
heavenly hands and my blood was boiling. The toil inside
my balls was working overtime. Handjobs were never so
supreme. And when she'd wash it all down with a mouth
minus the masticators, my mind relinquished reneged re-
buffed every virgin girl the good old boys in Amerika mighta
ever wanted to reproduce. My French-Canadian Come-
Queen lived for our time together and I did too. We were
totally going for each other's throats: me with my circum-
cised cock, she with her tantalizing tongue.

Once, when walking the park, we happened to cross paths
with a pack of fat old ladies from, yes, Quebec City. Iris knew
these contemporaries and hated their guts. Despised their
total mental/physical out-of-shapeness. She refused to ac-
knowledge their presence although their own refusal to hold
off on their hushed whispers of scandal made Iris nervous.
Even I, so lost in the boundary of her gaining-on-me grip,
heard one of the fat corpses say something in French that
sounded very nasty and deliberate. Iris was the only living
one among them and she knew this better than me.

One time, when we were just talking about life in general,
she told me about her home in Quebec City. Her two sons,
both around my age, were spending Christmas in Canada
and wouldn't be coming down to visit. She wasn't too sad
about this though because I was "filling in". You can
schizoanalyze these matters all you want, the plain truth of
the matter is that when I held onto her hand and took her for
a walk in the park, something unanalyzable took over both
of us, we became energized in a way no one can speak of.

Iris told me that one of her sons had taken over the basement in her house back in Quebec. One day last summer, she said, she went down to see how he was doing and found him smoking, how do you say, pot? YES, pot. Oui, oui, she continued, so I ask him if it's al-right I can try some too and he says oui-oui ma-ma, and so I try it and then I feel so good I go right to sleep.

It was then, sitting in a hotel bar, drinking beer and tomato juice (Iris' concoction), that I asked her if she'd like to blow some dope with me later.

"Blow some dope?"

"Oui, oui, smoke some pot, baby, with me, before…"

"…ah, oui-oui, tonight, it's okay?"

Of course it was okay. Anything was okay as long as she wanted it that way. All she had to do was ask, or hint at something. Besides, I had already bought my ticket to Mexico so we'd be forced apart (I guess I could have cancelled the trip to Mexico, but I felt smothered by Miami, which, despite Iris-beauty, always contaminated my sense of presence because of it being [literally being] my mother-city, so the trip was on no matter what, Iris would be there when I got back, at least I hoped she'd still be alive…)

Our days were numbered. So the idea of blowing some dope with ageless Iris was very appealing. She wanted to see a movie too. HAROLD AND MAUDE. No, just kidding, although having had already seen it back at U.C.L.A. film school did enter my mind on occasion. Iris was certainly much more beautiful than Ruth Gordon (although I'm not knocking Ruth, it's just that facts are facts) but there were some points of intersection in their personalities. They were THE REAL THING and their adventurous streaks were in direct opposition to the brainless conspiracy I now easily associate with MTV (femme fatales grinding in tightest lycra with jumpcuts to bare waists, pushed-out breasts, perfect asses, wild hair).

If Iris was a fetish, she was a being-fetish. The fact that she was old and had palms of gold with which she lubricated my performative projectile was beside the point. What we had was unconditional. All we asked of each other was total immersion in our frequent bursts of irresponsible sexual energy. The cliched motto she unwittingly turned into demonstrable actions was LIVE LIFE WHILE YOU STILL CAN. As for me, Iris, I now realize, was my death wish, plain and simple. I often imagined that I was fucking her to literal death (and that as soon as she died, I would die too). It was something teenyboppers never really had to offer me. It was always some other vice that the teenies went to right after we screwed. The closest one at hand (pot, coke, cig, drink, book, stereo, chewing gum, phone...). Iris, when we were through searching and destroying, would take her hands and play with her still-alive commodity.

I have a confession to make: I would eat her shit now that I know what I know. What I know is that she's dead and that she'll never resolve another day's full nutritional intake with the smooth release of her fecal matter. Knowing that makes me want it, makes me want it so bad I'm almost willing to resurrect her here in my memoirs just so that she may have the honors. But she's dead and I'm still wondering if she really meant what she said the last time I saw her. What she said was: "Next time you come to Miami, you will call me, yes?, and then I'll let you kill me..."

WHORE: A LOVE SONG

Jean Genet says:

...I wanted to swallow myself by opening my mouth very wide and turning it over my head so that it would take in my whole body, and then the Universe, until all that would remain of me would be a ball of eaten thing which little by little would be annihilated: that is how I see the end of the world.

This ball of eaten thing was what I had become. Precious few hours were left in the day where I could start scumming my way to the top of someone's burgeoning face, someone whom I not only desired for their melting sweetness, but someone whose enervating naivete caused monumental disruptions inside my body. With each passing quake of insurmountability processing itself deep inside my psyche, there came an aftershock of not being able to do anything. This overwhelming sense of powerlessness that superseded my deepest desire to transform my body into the most advanced technology ever to find its way through the darkest recesses of Amerika's censored imagination, left me feeling sad and empty.

Everywhere I went, I felt the need to question our absolute necessity as contemporary Men to continually place material gain over incessant genital licking. I was constantly throwing our dysfunctional culture into question: why hadn't the pleasure principle made itself the ground wire of my robotic brethren? What was it that Men wanted, or, more importantly, what didn't they want, and why?

Women, of course, wouldn't stand for it. Libido was calling and something inside their bodies was answering. The response was to go out into the sludge of post-industrial waste they called society and find a Man. A Man was a hard thing to find. They were mostly cocooning inside their home box offices trying to develop new configurations of market-able thought that would enable naive consumers to see themselves in a different light. The only exceptions were men who didn't care about the future and who never bought into the bullshit market economy they had been born into. These few men, universally seen as rare commodities, were usually transformed into whores who would have to beg or steal for a meal unless they hooked up with a wealthy wench who fell in love with them. Rita fell in love with me because I reminded her of her first lover, a writer, who she met in her undergraduate years at The University of Florida. I wasn't really in love with her but I did manage to find a way to enjoy having sex with her. I equated it with money. Since money was what everybody lacked and everybody wanted, and since she kept giving me all I needed as long as I bit her nipples gently sucking on them as if extracting some secret love potion from them, I sucked. I bit.

Rita wanted to come see my performance art show that was scheduled for tonight and although I wanted to say no, I couldn't. She could do anything she wanted. I would let her do anything she wanted to me in private or in public. She had no reservations about sharing me with her confidants. There were three friends who lived in town and two others who were still brave enough to fly the unfriendly skies to wher-ever young intelligent dick waited for them. I had some piss-poor musician-poet friends, contemporary Dionysian spirits, whom I thought of orgainizing into a working collective. The object would be to have a rotating crew of bright young whores whose cries of stallion verse while making love (having sex) would turn the moneyed madonnas mad with orgasms. Rita would have nothing of it. She said she wanted to keep it all in the family although I wasn't sure what she meant by that. I never saw her as family. The Mother With Cash connection was only a way for me to refer to her undoings of me. She was a far cry from my mother who would have never paid for it. (My dear mother, God rest her soul, *would* have accepted a cash payment for her own services should they be deemed necessary, *but pay for it?! NEVER!*)

Rita was very generous with me when it came to her friends. She was Queen Bee readily issuing slots of my time for the express purpose of making them (her friends) come. I never thought of myself as much of a lover and, in fact, never really was. (Anyone, if they fidget in the right place for the right amount of time, can make a cunt come, especially if the neural network backing it up is tempered with heavy doses of the latest anti-depressant drug.) Naturally, my embarking on this whore of a journey has given me the opportunity to improve my ability to make them come. Out of sheer boredom I've been forced to find ways to prolong their ecstatic agony. I call it agony because of the pain I hear in their voices as they let themselves go. It's those voices, the voices of animal spirits wrestling with the idiotic world they find themselves entrapped in, that make me continue the gallant enterprise of fanatical fidgeting. I am a fidgeter of whatever remains soft and sensitive in our brutal world. My digitals are composing this love song as I speak.

In preparing for tonight's art performance, I had my computer get in touch with everybody else's computer, daring them to come out and experience the rapture of minds becoming bodies again. *Bodies Partying* is what I titled the event, the entire release said

Bodies Partying

You can no longer represent yourself.
Hyphen-in-your-eye means a new way of looking at things.
Swallow yourself by opening your mouth wide and turning
it over your head so that you're nothing but the eaten thing.
Swollen externalities pervade your whore-o-scope.
Buy into the idea of selling yourself as a poetic gesture
worth a thousand comes.

I didn't ask for an RSVP nor did I say where it was happening since everybody knew where it would happen. If it happened. I didn't want to go. Why would they? I guess I did want to see who had the guts to go out and try to possess The Other. Especially since I was the Other. It was my last art performance spectacle some two years ago that I risked everything and not only showed up but did some ver weird shit. I was a raging lunatic whose nakedness and explicit references to fucking and coming and being a body erupting made many people freak. Most of the attitudes of the people who came out that particular time were laced with complacency. Home really *was* where the heart was and they all left it (the heart) right there (in the bedroom, the kitchen, the computer, the shitter). Why they came out one can only guess. Probably to see if they could go and come back without

blowing their whole existence. To blow your whole existence was really where it was at. That's what made an event
truly worth attending. It happened all the time. Reputations
depended on it. Someone would inevitably use the coming-
out experience as an excuse to explode. I did. Usually what
happens when you explode is that you either get assimilated
by an Institution (school, family, hospital, corporate death
factory) or someone present at your time of explosion sees
something they like and immediately wants to buy into it
and so they come up to you and try to convince you that they
can make the world a better place for you to co-exist in. Rita
did that for me. She came up to me and told me that she
thought I was very intelligent. She said she thought I was
very attractive. She said that she could make me very happy
and that I could make *her* happy too and that she'd take me
back to her enormous mountain house overlooking the city
where I'd have ample time to prove it. Prove what? (I
remember asking her this, I was so confused.) Prove to me
that you can make me happy (was her response). (My
confusion was now turning into simple lust with no thoughts
about how I got to the point I was at. She wanted me to prove
to her that I could make her happy. I had no idea who she was
but I did know how to make her happy even if I wasn't the
very best at it. The idea of a house turned me on. I needed a
house. A house was what motivated me just like it had
motivated my ancestors. My hard work had finally paid off.
I was going home. I was closer to death than I had ever
remembered being.)

Rita's friend Monette was flying in from New York and she
also wanted to attend the performance. I had had sex with
Monette once and it was a very strange experience for me.
The sex itself was great as usual. I say "as usual" because now

that I know almost all the tricks of the trade (some of which I've invented myself), it's pretty damn hard, no matter what the psychic state of The Other, not to make her come. There are things I can't even reveal they're so unknown and not worth risking my livelihood over.

The first and only time we had been together, Monette, who had just got a divorce from her corporate go-getter husband on grounds of his not understanding her desire to become a writer, had unthinkingly spilled herself all over me drenching me in the gaseous perfume of her catastrophic alliance. The stress on her face was so bundled up that the premature wrinkles rippling from her dark deadbrown eyes were like thick bulging veins popping out of her skin. She couldn't have been more than forty but looked a completely smoked-out 65.

It was obvious that she was spooked by my collective energy and wit. I'm sure it had a lot to do with the fact that I was very young yet still had a great deal of control over my language and said things that my body really felt. I said things to her like "sometimes when you come I feel like my whole world is being stripped of its artificial resonance". I said it like I meant it and instead of trembling in my hands like most of the others, she just looked at me like I was a totalitarian dick-energy sapping her of all attendant desires. She was becoming afraid of me and used this growing fear to create a dysfunctional relationship that would stop us from finding the love that might have been there. She called me a creep and said the only difference between me and an evil genius was that I wasn't close to being a genius. Then she kissed me long and hard eventually biting my tongue so brutally she ripped into the fleshy nerve and caused ripples of blood to pour out of my mouth. Instantly she became a child again, licking up the bloody red saliva with such voracity that I thought she was borderline vampire. "No," she explained to me, "I just wanted to taste the life of the man who stole me from myself." I thought I'd never see her again but here she was flying into town the night of the big performance.

I knew my own contribution to the *Bodies Partying* event would be much more tame than the last time I came out. It had to be. I was now part of the taken care of. I was a member of the kept. I slept in very late. I ate only organics. I wrote. I composed with my technologically advanced digitals feeling for attentive respondents. I was aerobically fit. I devised ways to insure myself that the woman who was in love with me stayed in love with me. I planned on reading a short-short with hardcore free-bop musical accompaniment. The short-short went

Smothered in the remote palace of Herself,
he prolonged the agony.

Moonlighting in derelict whoring, he
succumbed to the disembodiment of pleasure.

Eventually, they ripped into him with hatchets
and pieces of PCV pipe.

Set his hair on fire and threw him into
the cesspool that used to be a river.

Her recycled favors penetrated deep into
the city's darkened psyche.

A new lover was born.

He didn't know from where he came.

It didn't matter.

He was functional.

She was in love.

THE KAFKA CHRONICLES

Samsa found himself in a beautiful hotel suite with the woman of his dreams. She quietly removed her green silk dress, letting it drop to the floor like a disposable tissue one no longer had any use for. She snapped off her bra and pulled off her high heel shoes and stockings so that now she stood in front of him wearing nothing but her pink bikini underwear.

"Eat me," she said. Her tone was commanding yet still a whisper.

Samsa went down on his knees and put his hands on her taut thigh muscles. For a few seconds he just stuck his face against the bikini briefs breathing in the odor of her aura. He sensed the oncoming terrain of earthy flavors full of molten cheese and fuchsia rains. When his mind finally made itself up, when Gregor Samsa saw himself for who he really was, he stripped the body in front of him of its last remaining threads and quickly, insatiably, forced his tongue into the cul de sac of pussy that gloated before him.

He stayed right there in that bent sucking motion for twenty minutes. Then the woman who had fed him her curds and whey sat down beside him, kissed his cheek and told him to put her panties back on for her. He obeyed. She then asked him to help her on with her bra, which he did, and then, after she put her dress back on, she had him go back down on his knees and put her black high heel shoes on her.

"What about your stockings?" Samsa asked her.

"They're for you," she said. "I want you to put them over your head, to cover your face with them. Then I want you to walk out of this hotel with them still on your face. Don't worry about the room. I'll take care of it. You're a fool Samsa, a malleable construct who has no power over me and yet somehow still thinks he's got it made. I'll call you when I need you. Here—" and she handed him a fifty dollar bill and left the room.

"Bitch," Samsa muttered to himself. "Goddam bitch *owes* me. I'm worth so much more than that, so much more... "

Mandy Bauer was telling Crystal Geyser that not only did she know Gregor Samsa, she had had sex with him. "Only once," she said, "it was in the Kenmore Hotel just outside of Gramercy Park in New York City. He had just returned from Europe, was dead broke, had borrowed a hundred bucks from one of his last remaining friends, decided to take a room in the biggest shit-hole he could find. Ends up the shit-hole wasn't so big after all. Twice the size of a broom closet. Anyways, the Kenmore had an agreement with the Manhattan Health Club which was down in the renovated hotel basement, that any of the hotel's guests could use the club facilities. It was a safe deal for the health club because most of the guests were bug-infested transient types who would rather stay out in the cold wheezing and bleeding and drinking instead of kicking back and taking in a mentholated steam bath. To each his own, right? But Gregor, full of writing rigor and always interested in mixing up the staid scenery, utilizes the club regularly, right? So I'm just getting through this hellacious day out in the art network, I've been arranging a crack/coke deal for Drake Upstart who's now with Delilah Serenity who stole him from Aphrodite Rich, meanwhile Drake's having these conniptions where he starts leaking what appears to be a smelly blue gas from his nostrils, I'm getting sick just talking about it. *It really disgusts me,* but I just hold my breath and try to comfort him as best I can.

Amber Waves drops in and says the **doppleganger** isn't in till midnight. That means Drake'll have to wait. As soon as he hears this he goes crashing insane, rips off Amber's halter-top and starts sucking her nipples lost-man-in-the-desert-style. Amber's enormous oasis settles him down and now he's just whimpering in her cleavage, she's saying it's okay Drake, at least you've got Delilah. Meaning his show, of course! So I leave Amber with him and take off for the Manhattan Health Club. I mean, a little self-cleaning is in order, right? So I go for a long mentholated steam bath and that's when Gregor walks in. He's very shy. He can barely look at me. But he still manages to smile and takes a seat near me on the bench although his shy smile is a sly smile. He's implicating me in his crime and I don't even know him. I just have to put myself within his proximity and already he's having this strange effect on me. I came to get away from everything and now I'm totally engrossed in reading this guy's sly smile shy smile. Try saying that three times real fast: shy smile sly smile shy smile sly smile shy smile sly smile. You see? *He's still working on me and I'm already through with him!* Anyways, I'm starting to fantasize about who he is and what he's about. I mean he could be anybody. He could be an investment banker for Shearson-Lehman, he could be a bike messenger, he could be the ghost of Henry Miller. He could be nobody. But that's ridiculous, because I'm obviously getting turned on to some-body (or so I think). So I do the inevitable: I smile back. I know, Crystal, you're thinking, cheap slut, all the guys in the world after me and here I am picking up transient smut at the Kenmore, but I assure you that was not the case! This was different. I could tell. I mean no, I didn't have the results of his blood test in my hands, but something inside me ticked off a feeling that assured me he was clean. And after having spent an afternoon with that crack-addict pseudo-artist Drake Driphead, this guy seemed totally disease-free! I was sure of it!! I could just feel it! And Crystal, let's be honest here, you know how much feelings count for me. I don't let the media brainwash my cerebrum. So I did the obvious: I asked him his name. He said he was Gregor Samsa. I thought that a strange name indeed. But I didn't say anything to him. I didn't want to bug him about it. Besides, why exterminate the relationship before it even has a chance to begin! I was waiting for him to ask me my name but he never did. He seemed very content just sucking up the mentholated steam. He was obviously trying to open up his pores, his sinuses. He too was cleaning out. I could tell he was clean, trying to get even cleaner. Now Crystal, you know how my mind works, I can't control it sometimes. Don't forget: I was weaned on potential detonation. Culture's a sales pitch. I know that's a fact because I help sell it. Every day of my life I go out and try to sell the image of the artist as a worthwhile investment. Of course, speaking on behalf of myself, Mandy Bauer with the karma kandy eyes, I'll remind you that I'm still trying my damnedest to develop a transgressive video persona that I can flash before the idiot eyes of mass fascination. Amerika's battered psyche is on my side!! *They make me this way.* I'm not this way at all. I'm really not. I'm still the quiet little Episcopalian who got Bas-Mitzvahed at the age of thirty. Everything's so fucked up, Crystal, I, I almost feel as though I'll never survive. I mean why try and figure things out. Barbara Kruger, you know, she's got it down. One of her posters says EVERYTIME I HEAR THE WORD CULTURE / I REACH FOR MY CHECKBOOK. That's me, Crystal! She hit the nail right on the fucking head! I think every Nineties woman is this way. I'm talking impulse. I'm talking desire.

I'm talking the ability to wake up in the morning and suck the first cock that turns you on. Oh sure, I mean you could be cruising down Canal Street and all of a sudden you see some really hot blouse to go with that skirt you just bought last week and it's no problem, you flip out the plastic, you Do The Right Thing, and it's yours. You buy it. You buy it on impulse. It's great. No prob. You've done it before. It's safe. It doesn't talk back to you. It doesn't cheat on the side. It's not after your future inheritance. My clothes are my pets, I'll be the first one to admit it. No regrets here, it's life in a dark depeche mode. Something to wear to the opening. Lotta stares, lotta glares. You find out who your friends are. My friends are all s.o.b.'s. Rich jaded cunts. 'My, that looks lovely on you, where on earth did you find it?' Cunts. I have no use for them. They have no use for me either. *That's why we get along so well!* It's all we have. It's like constant dying but I don't want to get into that right now because I've been spending *my whole fucking day* dealing in death trying to keep the life-forces at bay. Meanwhile this hot guy in the bath gets up and leaves. *On impulse* I follow him out of the club and see that he goes straight to the elevator. He doesn't even bother taking a shower or changing his clothes. Obviously he's a hotel guest. But this shit-hole isn't even a hotel anymore. It's a crashpad for bugs and human figures molested by bugs. So I immediately find myself wanting to know more. I watch the elevator lights move up to the 11th floor and figure that since he's the only one who entered the elevator from the ground floor that that must be where he's staying. Just then a tall anorexic black woman with a face made in Eczema says 'You wanna know who that is?' Well, I tell her, I already know who it is: it's Gregor Samsa. 'Yes,' she says, ' but you don't know nothin'. Gregor ain't so easy to be known. He mysterious. He one sly motherfucker.' I asked her for her help. She said he was in room 1111. I thanked her and took the next elevator up. At this point I was no longer thinking. I wasn't capable of being anything, not even myself. Self had disappeared rather conveniently which is good I suppose. You work so hard to develop a creative concretized self and then out of nowhere you find that you don't even know you've lost it. You just don't know. The whole idea of knowing is down the tubes with the rest of your culture. *I can see this in my art.* But maybe I'm just blinding myself to the outer resources. Plenty of people I know are using the system to their own advantage. Then again, maybe the people I know and come into contact with are at an extreme advantage when it comes to using the system. I don't know, I don't want to think about it. So I don't. I knock on the door. I hear his voice say hello. The smell of sweet ganja seeping from underneath his door rising into my nostrils. It smells wonderful. Especially after having been overexposed to Drake's dreary blue gas which I'll find out later is the artist decomposing. I pause for a few seconds because I don't know what to say although I'm still not thinking I'm just waiting for the right words to rise up into my throat so that I can get him to open the door. 'It's me,' I say, 'we just met in the steam bath.' He opens the door. The room is filled with exhaled sinsemilla. His eyes are glazed green vermin as innocent as I've ever seen. I'm no longer myself. I'm just a low-priced whore who happens to be surviving in the multi-national world's capitol city. I ask him if I can come in and he says, Sure, moves out of the way. The room, like I say, is about the size of two broom closets. One half is where he parks his bike. The other half has his single bed and a night table with a phone on it. Next to the phone is the half-smoked joint and an open notebook full of scribble. He's probably writing all this down as I speak. It doesn't matter what happens next but I'll tell you anyway. I become an expert masseuse. I tell him that that's my background and that I noticed in the steam bath that he seemed a little tense. Would he like a rub-down? He says the one word he knows best. He says 'Sure'. He lays on his stomach on the bed. He's still wearing his bright yellow swimtrunks, the ones he wore in the bath. I ask him if he'd mind it if I pulled them off. He said no and lifted his torso up off the bed so I could reach underneath him and pull them off. He had a really nice ass. Hard as a fucking rock. The black girl who works the hotel, her voice, entered my mind. She had said that he was mysterious. A sly motherfucker who wasn't easy to know. The more I heard her words the more I felt myself becoming something like her. A junky black whore who worked the Kenmore. I started feeling more like the real me too. This was who I was. Networker by day, whore by night. The idea of mixing night and day turned me on. I was fantasizing that every move I made was being broadcast to all of Amerika. I was Amerika's whore, going down on her Native Son. I was kneading Gregor's flesh with as much subtle force and love-energy as I could muster, paying particular attention to his hard skinny ass. The more I concentrated on his ass the more I desired it. I was losing myself again but this time I was losing myself as somebody else. It was easier to handle. I was the black chick losing herself tonguing deep inside the crack of his beautiful white ass licking up whatever remains of scummy shit lodged up inside it. I was no longer I, I was "I", something in constant flux, a metamorph sucking on chunks of smooth rumperstiltskin. I was lifting his ass up a little so that my tongue could reach up and over to his hairy balls which were the biggest balls I had ever seen. I got so wound up by it all that I almost couldn't breathe. I was tingling. I told him to turn over. He didn't respond. I asked him if he would please turn over so that I could massage the front of his body. He made a noise like he was just getting up in the morning and turned over. His dick was hard. Big Blue. I immediately started sucking him off. I knew my tongue had sharp little hairs and teeth all over it. I was special. Mama always said I was special. I had my special trick. I called it Cilia With A Kiss. My microscopic tongue hairs subtly bit his sensitive dick as I deepthroated him all the way down his enormous shaft. I realized this must be new and exhilarating for him but I checked to make sure anyway. I asked him if I was hurting him. It was the first time I had really looked into his eyes since entering the room. His light green beamers were steaming and his hair was curlier than it had been in the steambath. His face was wet with accumulated moisture. The sly smile shy smile was now a grimaced expression part pain part intense pleasure. I looked at him waiting for his response. A positive signal and I'd continue to lose myself in the purest act of fiction I could possibly make for myself. He managed to extol my performance in one word: 'great'. I continued the raging suck-off until he couldn't hold back his steamy come anymore. What seemed like floods of sticky bittersweet sperm came inside me and I, who never have trouble swallowing, felt overwhelmed by his abundance. For the first time in my life, I choked. But before it could drip out of my mouth and onto the sheets, I recovered my senses and made sure it all went down. He was looking into my eyes and obviously felt relieved. He seemed very clear. With his sperm still melting in my mouth, I got up, still staring at him in the eyes. I didn't know what to do. Or say. But I instinctively left it all open by mumbling 'This one's on me.' Then I left."

Samsa makes his move and doses on more stimulation. In all his dreams he's being happily nullified by the forces outside himself. His polymorphous perversity entitles him to multi-orgasmic experiences full of gushing organic juices filling the mouths of babes. These sexual proclivities are being broadcast live via satellite to all free countries around the globe. Sometimes he sees himself in old reruns playing the role of preeminent rock and roller who gets any chick he wants. Right now his latest music video is being segued into the MTV rock-around-the-clock rotation. He's a Love God, a carefully created icon who knows how to manage his entrepreneurial hustle.

All of a sudden the simulated experience of being someone who he's not becomes too much to handle. He wakes up and finds himself strapped to the bed. CIA bugs inserted in all his organs he's being read by every amateur critic the bureaucracy produces. An authoritarian voice comes blaring through the multi-national superstate's implanted speakers. It says:

"Wake up Samsa, it's time to go to work!"

His whole body shakes as the new pop anthem plays its catchy phrases and unforgettable hooks force him to unstrap himself and get his ass out of bed so that he can crawl to the shower.

"This early morning wake-up call is being sponsored by…"

The daily news comes blasting from the speakers in perfect comedy shtick delivery although the announcer (whose voice may not be real) doesn't wait for his laughs:

"The swollen slobbering hierarchy rams its pusillanimous predator into her automotive concave and bureaucratic love codes get tapped on her nymphomaniacal wires.

"The frequency rate increases exponentially as she goes down on me and then after swallowing the entire Big Board immediately opens up her legs allowing all potential USA-dollars to get distributed throughout the fiber optic network.

"According to The State Department, the reactivation of certain buzzwords in cellular biophonetic theory will now lead to an epidemic of epidermic needle infiltration inside most GM cars despite earnest attempts by GM to recall all hairy ignition switches and flaming clit revolvers that have been known to rev up potentially explosive pseudo-political transmissions.

"In Tokyo, lubricants of total immersion cause labia lips to squeeze.

"U.N. Peace Command sanctions fossil fuels while antediluvian tongue spills its Bedouin drool. As black spittle seeps out from her cut gums, a call to war has apparently recast the rhetoric of appearance.

"Meanwhile, inflation slips inside the back door and brutally drills her ass for more crude. An expert on continental cornholing says domestic reproduction is at an all-time low and that all turtle-snappin' pussy wasting away in the Texas region is now on alert for possible remission. Dormant Dora Denaturally was quoted as saying 'All you boys better git ya selves on down here cuz I'm achin' for the takin'..."

"Gushing diarrhea at the mouth leads mad dictator astray while laymen spray chemical by-products all over the Situationist's anarchic exhibition. The National Council On the Arts claims 45 casualties and says, 'If this doesn't affect Dow, nothing will.'

"An apocalypse of orgasms beads the air while the flames of femme fatales flee in terror."

Gregor simulated his death by going back to the typewriter and making things up as he went along. He spontaneously created himself while simultaneously undoing himself so that what you had left was a transient glow, a wafer thin line of desire dressed up in the latest perspiration-wicking athletic wear Amerikan money could buy. He was no longer an outcast. He was Down and In, Up and Coming, Off and Running. He was all Presence. A thought was rolling through his head: let it be first of all by their presence that objects and gestures establish themselves...He took a deep breath. The typewriter was buzzing with action, inviting him to join in the fun.

Technology was shooting him right between the eyes. Christmas was just around the corner and his mother was going insane trying to light the menorah candles. She ended up setting the Hanukkah bush on fire and Gregor, watching old reruns of The Sonny and Cher show, ran to her assistance.

"Oh God," said Gregor.

The burning Hanukkah bush spoke back to him.

"Please," said the bush, "don't give me that God crap, just get the fire extinguisher and put me out of my misery."

Gregor went in search of the readily accessible fire extinguisher but it was nowhere to be found. His mother, meanwhile, had run from the Miami Beach condo in hysterics. She was in a tattered peach bathrobe with an ancient *schmata* on her head. Gregor, looking out the sliding glass door at the back entrance to the condo, saw his mom run uncontrollably toward the swimming pool. She was picking up speed as she approached the water and for some ungodly reason, she kept going at full speed when she hit the water so that she ended up running across half the pool's length before allowing the better part of herself to take over and sink her into the deep end.

She didn't know how to swim. She had lived in Miami Bitch all her life but swimming was out of the question. Are you kidding? That would mean she'd have to get wet. Why get wet when you have showers for that? Or so the logic went. But there was no logic gonna save the yenta from drowning so Gregor, forgetting about the burning bush as it spread to the sofa and the Lay-Z-Boy chair, ran out to save his mom from a death spiked with chlorine.

He dove into the pool but his mom was gone. There was a floating life-size mom made of plastic. He pulled the dummy mommy out of the water and without thinking ran with it back to the condo. His adrenalin was flowing so intensely that it started slowly seeping out of his penis hole. Soon his adrenalin was literally pouring out of his penis hole so he pulled off his shorts and on instinct forced the gushing penis-head into the dummy mommy's mouth where an opening the size of a wooden nickel suddenly appeared. Once the dummy mommy was filled with his adrenalin he then started spraying it on the fire. He didn't put the fire out but he did manage to contain it until the firemen came bursting through the front door and finished the job.

"What exactly happened?" asked the fire chief once the fire was completely out and the charred remains of Gregor's existence blew around the place in a warm sea breeze.

"I don't have any idea," said Gregor, "I don't even know where this place is."

Transient hype-star feeding off the quick-change scenery of somebody else's memory gone blank, G left the typewriter and went out for a swim. Later he'd go to the mall and finish his Xmas shopping.

Somewhere in Boulder, Colorado, his sweet sister, the tainted Barbarella, painted her way back onto his canvas-mind, and he told her her timing was perfect. She seemed less timid than the last time he saw her. Apparently she had just gone to see his experiential psychologist. When Gregor asked her if Quasar, the experiential psychologist, assisted her in finding her roots, Barb simply stated that Quasar was emphatically doing nothing of the sort and had, in fact, deregulated the level playing field so that Barb could *create* a whole new network of underground wiring to feed off of. Gregor nodded in understanding.

She was lush and lucid. The snow she dripped in was glistening on her face, God's icy come melting both in her mouth and in her hands. She wasn't really dressed for the weather. Some unforeseen arctic blast had collided with Gulf of Mexico moisture causing severe upslope conditions. It was one of those days when you wondered what the fuck you were doing in such an unpredictable environment and cursed the day you moved here. But Barb's barbaric beauty and easygoing headtrip made things better. Much better.

"My eyes hurt," she said to her older bro. "Would you gently massage them for me?"

Gregor's response was ineffable. An erotic sign language using only the tip of his tongue. Running through the letters of the alphabet, he flicked his budding red nerve over her eyes. In this senseless tracing of instantaneous ecstasy, he purveyed enough love-energy to ignite the surface tension laced across her body. The near-fractal lacework that had somehow made her entrance seem so strong and stable was now coming apart at the seams. Seems as though his sensual dynamic, totally out of his control and part of his physical make-up, was conscientiously turning her aura of aggression into an endless string of orgasmic opportunities. The pin-plug method wasn't out of the question but they both preferred utilizing the mechanism on batteries. It was good practice. In case of emergencies. Was this an emergency?

Gypsy mouth traversing the parent culture *in absentia*.

Immediate realignment with previous vestige of errone-ous self zoning out on liquid dementia.

Psychopharmokinetic reaction to the sun reflecting off the snow while he simulates a rock and roll self catching rays inside the beach of her viscous fluid.

THIS IS THE HOUSE THAT FRANZ BUILT.

Psychotic energy transforming the self into a living pest.

Indigents indigenous to the area being scrawled on the wall.

He crawls on top of her.

Mutters the words *gimme shelter*.

AND FRANZ MADE GREGOR IN HIS OWN IMAGE. Fetish subordination? What was she really after? He had just woken up. Drank a quick cup of homemade espresso, threw on his winter longjohns and everything else meant to retain his heat. Was walking toward the university campus, waiting at a red light. Busy intersection. Felt a gentle tugging at his thinsulate jacket sleeve. Turned a little to the left and saw her standing there. She was smiling like she had known him for years and was happy as all hell to see him (again). She kept rolling her eyes up at him the way some groupies who come out to his performance art shows do. Being the honorable gent that he was, he smiled back and said, "Hey". She brushed up against him and asked him if he'd take off his shades so that she could really see him. It was cold and he had to take his hands out of his coat pockets, pull off his waterproof mittens and wool-lined gloves to free a hand so he could take off his wraparound shades. There they were, his eyes/her eyes; as soon as they made contact she said "meeting of the minds," and he immediately replied, "minds meet." The light changed and he began to shift his body weight and momentum toward the street but she held onto his sleeve with a little more force than he expected and in an extraterrestrial way she emitted an aura of fuck-me-hard sensuality. He was used to this sort of thing. The performance art shows. The university readings. The occasional libido-inmixing shaking him up at a party, in a cafe. Hers was an energy that coated him in potential bliss. It was still first thing in the morning and he was writing it all off as hypnogogic hallucination with a little street theater thrown in for excitement. But she was hardcore serious about pursuing this potential bliss thing for as long as he'd let her. The light changed again and this time she knew she had to let him make his move across the street. If he waited there at the intersection for one more light he might explode. His cock was hard and bursting inside his pants. He wondered what he could possibly say or do to convey to her his deep affection for her instinctive measures. Instinctive in that they were hers. She wasn't acting in a prefabricated way. She wasn't coming on like a technical manual. She was a woman, he thought, a woman who, for some reason (or total lack thereof), felt bold and confident enough to come on to him like this. This wasn't the 60's. She wasn't going to bring him back to her hip hang-out pad and turn him on to all her girlfriends who were bored and smoking dope and looking for their next willing victim. Or was she? No. Definitely not (although it sounds exciting). It was the 90's. The 80's passed by without anything so much as a minor awakening. He was so lulled by the sleepwalking syndrome that even today, lost in the dreams of last night's festive orgies, he couldn't possibly have anticipated this sort of thing happening to him on the street first thing in the morning. And why was he going onto campus anyway? He wasn't a student per se. Student of life, sure. But no classes being taken, none being taught. He was an intruder. He had no real reason for being there. Maybe he was looking for some action? So early in the morning? He should have been in bed bundled up in blankets putting everything off until tomorrow. "Can I hold your hand," she asked him as they crossed the street. Her voice was like a little girl's, real innocent. Although he started getting a different vibe from her now, not so much little girl lost-in-space, more like young adult on-the-verge-of-suicide madness. Why was she fishing around in his coat pocket looking for his hand which was keeping him warm and going nowhere? Was this some kind of fetish? Was he her fetish? He'd had hand fetishes before. He'd had every kind of fetish before. The thing that always made the fetish work, the thing that turned him on right now as he felt his cock stir inside the polypro underwear, was the fact that the particular body part he was craving was attached to a total stranger. That was the real fetish right there. Her anonymity. A strange college woman, no more than twenty-four years old, holding onto his cock, either in her hand or in her mouth, maybe in her cunt, perhaps up her enormously attractive ass. The idea of getting laid all of a sudden appealed to him. "Here," he said, sending their body weight toward the left. "Let's go this way." She had put her arm in the opening his hand-in-pocket had provided. She was lonely and desperate for his affection, his, Gregor, our man lost in the wilderness of his potential bliss. He was still stirring down below inside the polypro, but his mind was where all the action shifted to. He was improvising a whole disposition of invisible screens to lose himself in. The makeshift TV image he had made of himself was now watering at the edges. The sun was barely out but it was just hot enough to start melting the snow. They were walking on thin ice, getting their feet wet. "Where are you taking me?," she asked him. "Where do you want to go," he asked back, not too sure where he wanted to take her, not too sure if taking her on was really the right thing at all. Then he said: "We're limited—we're on foot." There was a pause.

He couldn't take her home. The privacy factor. The piracy factor. His absconding souls schematics was not for public viewing, least of all his Keeper, their out of town guests, the animals. No, now was the time for him to take on that role he so eagerly sought to portray, that of the Invisible Man whose glowing libido made him the Confidence Man. Now if only he could find a place to bang her. After all, that's what this is all about, isn't it? There might be many of the key elements one needs to incorporate the sexual topos into the "story", that is to say Pleasure, Desire, Bliss, Experience and even the value of drifting into the intractable so as to intensify the protagonist's ineptitude at setting clearly focused priorities, but the bottom line here is and always will be Gregor Samsa getting laid as much as anybody, maybe more. What else was there to live for? The Sexual Revolution wasn't necessarily back as it once was, no, that was for sure, but his personalized improvisation of something close to it was, to him, an assault on the shallow values of his mindless generation climbing naked up the broken rungs of the corporate ladder. He didn't want to fuck this bored semi-crackpot college woman just to get his rocks off, no, he wanted to fuck her because fucking her was fucking the world, was telling the whole world that it was time to wake up and smell the coffee. If waiting for the light to change was how long it took him to reenact a recurring desire to change the world, then by God he'd have to do his civil duty and take this strange lass under his wing making sure to rail her completely out of her head, flood of loco motives moving off track into schizo serene pastures of pleasure. Kiss her (a voice in his head whispered to him). He kissed her. They were on campus, near the fountain where all the main traffic moved through. A thought raced through his mind that he might run into somebody he knew, or maybe someone who knew his Keeper. And they'd see him walking with this other woman whose arm was snugly wrapped inside his. And they'd think that he was fooling around, or they'd reaffirm what they already knew about him, or they'd just wonder who she was, or, best of all, they wouldn't care about him or his situation at all. They would have no idea what circumstance had brought them together. He felt the need to duck out immediately so he mentioned the "Where to?" to her again. She said: "The biology lab." "The biology lab?" "Yes," she said. She had the look of a baglady who was anything but reality-grounded. "The biology lab is my self," she said. "The biology lab is your self?" Her eyes went hazy and her body jerked in uncontrollable reaction. He obviously didn't pick up on her intense vibes. She needed to know he was serious about all this. He picked up on his mistake, his missed note, and said, "The laboratory of your soul," and she flashed him that same smile she had when she first tugged at him. "Love is better than pain," she said and he thought her line to be too cliched to respond to but his cock was still stirring and he figured what the fuck, love really is better than pain, but why mention it? At this point the idea of inflicting a kind of emotional pain on her was maybe the best way out of this jam he had now decided he had gotten himself into. Her lines were becoming too arbitrary and banal. She was just another slum-bunny who fanagled enough financial aid out of the system to keep her going for a few years. She was slightly mad or worse than that she was an absolute loon tune. She'd take six years to get a B.A. in Sociology and then she'd help displaced Latin Americans beat the system in central California. She'd take on a lover whose past was unknown to her. He'd be, among other things, a rapist, child molester, bank embezzler, armed robber and crack dealer. She'd be carrying his baby just as he went to prison. The baby would be born into a world full of organics. TV would be a really good thing to watch. Mind-altering drugs would be the fashion. You would walk down the street feeling groovy and all of a sudden, waiting at a stoplight, a woman would come up to you and let you know exactly how she felt about you (or what she fantasized was you). She'd be totally together and terribly excited about getting it on with you. She'd tell you this and you'd ask her where should we go and she'd jingle a set of keys saying the biology lab. You'd say that you thought the lab was closed for finals week and she'd get a seductive grin on her face and say Yes, I know, exactly. With tubes flying everywhere, the two of you would learn about each other's burning anatomy...

Now when I walk around at lunchtime I remember the greatest party of my life thrown by King Bohemia in his enormous Buddha house on the hill near Chautauqua. Everyone who was anyone was there: Milan, Zdenek, Eda, Vaclav, Jan, Eva, Franz and Mark. We were playing poker with food stamps and dots of black Leb Eva had smuggled in from Amsterdam. Nile was in town and had provided us all with mounds of purple haze. Katherine brought over her excess baggage filled with the kind of jocular pus only pinheads like me would enjoy seeping out from underneath her sumptuous skin. Mary was open about not feeling the need to bring anything at all. She said she had leeched off the many for far too long and couldn't bear the thought that she might have to start giving it all back so she wouldn't even think about it. Why think about it when you could just as easily wear it, she said to Franz and pinched his cheek. Franz wouldn't respond. He was too busy noshing on King Bohemia's great spread. He spent a particularly long time smearing vege pate on stoneground whole wheat crackers. After having *chazered* half the crackers, Franz tilted his head toward the ceiling and in a loud commanding voice told everybody that *he* was the life of the party and to prove it he took a broken cracker and proceeded to cut himself just above the wrist. He started spinning twisting and contorting as if blood was coming out in spurts and Nurze came over to put his miserable life back in order. Franz dug this immensely. He'd always been attracted to Nurze but didn't really have the balls to tell her. Nurze was telling him that he should know better than to do this but Franz was in the process of losing consciousness and couldn't relate to what she was saying to him. His aura was dimming toward total darkness. This "dematerialization" of the subject-matter (his self or self-pity) was just the thing the women at the party were after. All the comrades, no matter how much they hated to admit it, agreed. Franz-baby had his nut together. It was all a matter of disintegrating. Gracefully. If he could blast his message home then softly fade out into a mass of living silence without the slightest mistake (as was his case: he was a perfectionist), the women would go googoo over him. Mary & Eva & Ana & Alexandria all found their way over to the red beanbag where he was sprawled out toking on megadots of the black Leb occasionally chasing them with shots of Pilsner Urquell (he used to always make mention of the fact that to drink the pilsner in shots was *much* more effective than drinking it slowly out of the bottle). He was passing around the pipe and pouring shots into all the women's shot glasses rousing attention arousing erotic tension. Within minutes they were all happily stupored by the ecstasy that was nudging the moment. Mary was the first to dig in. She unbuttoned his starched white collar shirt and began caressing his tits. You hairy boy, she said, and that got Eva interested in having some fun too. Eva had a tremendous weakness for hairy chests. Hairy anything really. She even found herself turned on by the hanging nostril hairs coming out of Franz's hooked nose. She took her long fingernails and pinched his nosehairs as if she were playing, then, as if inspired, she pulled them as hard as she could, ripping them out of his nose. The pain was excruciating and Franz screamed at the top of his lungs. Everyone laughed because they were so smashed on the party favors supplied by the collective. But the pain was horrible and Franz swore to take revenge on the evil cunt who thought she could get away with it. Eva, being somewhat sado-maso and open to all kinds of experimenta-tion, told Franz that if he was really pissed off at her and wanted to get even, he should bite into her pubic hairs and pull them out with his teeth. Alexandria immediately egged him on because she had always wanted to see Eva's cunt. Alexandria, who had contracted a weird kind of sexual phobia early in her youth, was totally eroticized by Eva. She saw her as a hot Mother-figure. She had no explanation for it, since, for the better part of her life, she had absolutely no interest in anything sexually related. The thought of a kiss would make her stomach spin in mortal anguish. She'd rather die than kiss. Or so she thought (whenever the choice presented itself to her). Eva's being, her being there, with her skirt lifted and her panties pulled off, caused a life-bearing transformation within Alexandria's psyche that made her want to go down and do the biting/pulling herself. She told Franz that he better hurry up and start accessing this Queen of Bohemia or she'd rip into her herself. Franz relented. He went down and started licking Eva's clit. He wasn't into causing her or anyone else any pain. He was into personify-ing the pleasure principle to the max. His mind went lax and the body-eternal warped around the edges of her cunt. He was losing himself. He was finding himself. He was juicing herself. *He is herself de-defined.* He was no longer self-pity. *He was caught in a landslide of come* as it poured down the mountain right into his face. Everyone applauded his laud-able performance and Eva swore she broke her own personal record for Most Intense Come In A Single Sucking Session. King Bohemia said *the party's just begun* as he ran around the partyroom in nothing but his longjohns, all the dogs and goats running after him. Milan took out his video camera and began shooting the festivities and this, in turn, turned Katherine on. Nobody really knew Katherine that well. Her well was said to have run dry. But the video camera on automatic pilot as Milan ushered out drunken commands insisting on the pornographic positioning of all the players blew her mind. Maybe it was his thick Czech accent. Whatever it was, she felt the warm wetness of days gone by start to puddle up inside her athletic underwear and she grabbed hold of the first male arm she could find. That was me. Gregor Samsa. The guy supposedly responsible for making all of this happen. I was lost in a haze of hash and beer trying to figure out my role in all of this. I was just another Amerikan dissident writer who had seen the best minds of his generation sold to the bureaucratic nightmare world of dead data and all its surrealistic posturing. Katherine pulled me over to the corner of the room and asked me to feel her crotch. She was soaked. "My wet debris is only for thee," she smiled and I, noticing that the last beer was in fact *the* last beer, told her my cottonmouth was worse than Canyonlands in July, that her warm wet oasis of pleasure was just my cup of tea. I'd take it straight. No milk, no honey. Just pure dope. By the time I had said all this to her (not too long a time had passed but I was on hash-time, I was preempted), Vaclav had set up the movie projector and everyone had huddled in front of the screen. He yelled out at us to come on over and watch the movie, *the revolution*. Start without us, is what Katherine yelled back and so they did. Kat's creamy pilsner had quite a head on it. It had a most sobering effect...

Eric Konigsberg was a member of the biologic underclass. He had been diagnosed as having AIDS and this in turn destroyed his potential success as a composer of New Age music. He went to his old friend Gregor Samsa for some pity but all Gregor had was a bowl of jism.

"Here," said Gregor, "this jism is my sexual prism. Rainbow juices flow from me. My own gene pool manipulation has enabled me to put off the inevitable. Eugenics is the only thing that matters. Master race dominates me. Human experience all gone. We're One."

Eric broke down crying big eyedrops of self-pity.

"Stop it," said Gregor. "you're polluting the gene pool. Face reality, chimpanzee. We humans tend to believe in our biological determinism. My jism is my determinism. It's the sorcerer's siphoned off sexual glue. I wish I could help you but you just don't fit into our optimal genetic strategies. You're unemployable, uneducated, uninsured. What could I possibly do with you? Right now we're busy decentralizing our entire operation. Once we've successfully broken down the constricting nucleus of activity, then we can refocus our attention on profitability. That's where it's at Jack. Your piddling problems are useless to me. Useless."

Eric gained composure. He looked in Gregor's eyes and saw all human experience going down the tubes. He wanted to kill him. He wanted to kiss him. He wanted to be him.

Instead, he took the bowl of jism and wolfed it down in one gulp. Pieces of stringy sperm dripped out the side of his mouth. He looked at Gregor, his eyes dopey and his tongue dangling like an overworked dog.

"I guess you expect miracles," continued Gregor, not noticing what was happening around him. "There are three things I'm concerned about right now: first, your financial data profile. You're an idiot musician who thinks he's more sensitive to the human condition than even me. That's just utter bullshit. Second: what are my investment objectives? To take everything I've accumulated over the years and put it into ratty-ass socialist projects being composed by weird jew artists who suffer from diseases worse than t.b.? There just ain't no way in hell I'm gonna do it, Pal, no way in hell. Third: what is my level of risk tolerance? Obviously not as high as yours. You just drank a soup bowl's worth of my creepy come. God knows what kinds of death might be hanging out in there. You'll do anything for a dollar. What scum. And you have the nerve to call me your friend. Get out of my face. You're too much of a risk."

As soon as Eric Konigsberg left, Gregor picked up his soup bowl and licked it clean. The rainbow forming over his eyes turned neon and transmitted itself live via satellite. The whole world tuned in.

12/22/89

Bataille wrote "I write not to be mad." Me too. Although I'm not really mad. I'm angry. I'm very upset. I have a (perennial) bone to pick. In one sense, I feel like telling you, my reader, my best friend, the only one I can trust, to kindly take these insignificant writings away from me. Properly dispose of them (please). Why not burn them?

The pages themselves are burning already. Fanning the flames of Desire, I am the Mother of Necessity. But Necessity is taking me over. She's really too much. I can no longer see myself as Presence. The cloudy needs that hang over my eyes and create a kind of haze for my mobilized imagination to get lost in, keep me separated from the person I many times feel I ought to get to know. I'm now wondering, like all thinking minds wonder at one time or another, who am "I"? This question continues to nag me despite the fact that a recent surplus of delicately postured flesh has somehow made its way toward me and afforded me the opportunity to knead more than I could ever hope for in one lifetime.

My burden has been blissfully carried along for almost three decades, each year finding a better, more efficient way to transgress the proprieties of my societal situation, and, to be quite honest and upfront with you, I'm getting very tired of dallying in these useless forms trying to signal to you through the flames. My preference, all of a sudden, is to just dreamscape a different kind of scapegoat, a totally Other being-thing that might approximate the feeling of utter love-consciousness I find myself becoming.

The last thing I want to do is sound all self-centered and ego-intensified. Leave that to the philosophers, the post-structuralists or whoever else happens to be parading thoughts down our guttural streets. The fact is, like many who now have difficulty bringing home the bacon while simulta-neously engaging themselves in acts of writing, I too am the slightly mad English major whose radical (pre)disposition has got him totally wrapped up in figuring out (via experi-mentation) what in bloody hell this "me" thing is all about.

I don't understand the Movement of History. Prague is opening itself up to a dissident writer as President. Amerika votes in B-grade movie actors whose lines are written by commercial ad-copy writers. The engineering of human consent is now something we come to expect from our leaders. TV's a concentration camp. It concentrates on distracting you from finding out what a "me" is all about. It's pure camp. It's taking your eyelids off with a pair of pliers and using them for hairbrushes. It's bringing home the revolu-tion, live, via satellite.

The "miracle" now sweeping through the Motherland transforms all the great writers' words into an experiential energy guaranteed to blow the minds of people everywhere. My fellow Czechs are starting to pervade the consciousness of frustrated thinkers all throughout the West. It's not a communist energy they're sensing, it's not a kapitalist en-ergy, it's not even a democratic energy although for lack of better that's what they're calling it. Rather, it's an energy there's no word for. No term could possibly relate to you the feelings that are being transcribed by the Global Consciousness at this very moment. Yet the signifying madness created by the performance of this energy has got most people in this world going absolutely crazy. Chaos reigns supreme. Something's bound to explode.

12/23/89

The walls are being torn down. My loving F. called today to tell me that Florida had four inches of snow. Mention of the Greenhouse Effect. Mention of the eastern bloc of ice now melting. Mention of the heavy stress load encumbering the young minds squashed by The System. Mention of Japan our Slavemaster. Mention of our changing role in all of this. Mention of escaping Amerika, finding peace & solace & maybe more excitement in the regional theater somewhere in Czechoslovakia or Hungary or Poland. Mention of having to work for peanuts while the top-dogs get their $500,000 bonuses not to mention unconditional loans from their Savings and Loans cronies who can't wait to see their ships go under. Meanwhile, F., poor thing, got called into her boss' office only to be reminded that times are tough, raises are out of the question, best to stay on the ball and don't screw up, plenty of others out there just aching to walk in and replace you, thank you for all your help, Merry Xmas.

The new decade around the corner, the next millennia closer than ever, walls tumbling down & they expect us to put up with shit? Are they out of their fucking minds? What's worse, there's nothing we can do. Nothing but stay put and work. We can dream about getting out and maybe one day our government will let us go to school and get a good education. Maybe we'll see the day when a National Health Care program makes it possible for every citizen to receive the proper medical attention he or she might need in order to survive on this lovely planet. Maybe.

They want me to Just Say No to drugs and remain abstinent because sex is bad for me and can ruin my life but then they feed me highly toxic contaminants via the foodchain and turn my home into a radioactive wasteland to burn up in. They tell me only dopes smoke dope and eating female genitalia will kill me but then they put a brown cloud over my city and expect me to purify my holy Amerikan spirit by breathing in the thick corrosive air. I told F. that we *have* to get out. She reminded me that there's nowhere to escape *to*. Japan was worse off than us when it came to pollutants. Their cost of living was astronomical. The eastern bloc of ice melting on the scene of dying communism is just now starting to find out about the limited alternatives available to it and for us to go there would most definitely be a step *down* in standard of living. Gypsy transience and hardcore aesthetic radicalism seem too preposterous for consumer Amerika. Better to join the Men who've joined the Army. Better to kill the poor and go gaga over the rich. Rape the heart and soul of countries all around the world so that the dark aboriginal spirit that lurks within the heart of Men can reissue experience at a price heretofore unheard of. The new price is right!! Buy now / buy this / buy me / I'm this.

12/23/89 (later)

I've been walking around Boulder wondering about Prague. It's true, Amerika as it might have been envisioned from the Old Country in the beginning of the century is not what it's made out to be. Now it's the end of the century and things are turning upside-down. A dissident writer is President of all Czechs. I wish I could go back to my fellow Czechs and tell them all I know. It may not be much but that's okay: what I have to say comes from deep inside my heart. They will listen to me. My rap will be gallantly opposed to everything that tries to invade my private creative self.

Walking around Boulder I ventured into the monstrous healthfood supermarket, one of a kind anywhere in Amerika, and noticed that they had expanded once again. Their new marketing strategies are aimed at people like me. Young, white and totally turned on by the display of beautiful organic produce. I should be frequenting this place regularly. I'll take part in their organic juices (carrot, orange, grapefruit, beet, celery, spinach, wheatgrass, etc.), their fruit smoothies, their excessively healthy and delicious everything. I'll even wait in long lines if I have to.

I must tell my fellow creators back in Prague about all of this. I must tell them about Gore-Tex. I must tell them about Patagonia. I'll tell them about everything although they'll try to discourage me from talking too much about the pop culture. It doesn't really fascinate them. It's the trendy new products they want to have access to. Organic stoneground blue corn chips. Organic tomatillo salsa. Tofu fudge brownies. I will bring all of it back with me, safely kept in the far reaches of my imagination so that the customs officials here in Amerika have no chance of detecting my entrepreneurial armory. I'll make a fortune.

Companion compadres come closer. Curate careful creation. Crush communist cronies, crush. One slip and the trip

explodes

reneges on all artificially-inflated value. Once upon her time schemes places went somewhere, had excess openmindedness derived from carefree nonchalant doesn't matter anyway. Attitude spoken of earlier. Before. When we were talking about the other way of doing. Things we one time would have easily. But now with the field of limitations forced upon us no longer able. To make a clean escape since nowhere. To go would seem futile but maybe. Fun why not? Just for the fuck of. It better than us?

She takes hold of him and they start the wander. Lust her whole security spirit on the line because of the dread. Propaganda manifesting TV mediated foreplay causing newly accessed. Information processed a chance to include the establishment perspective in all our daily meals. Where the hormonal injection chemically alters our perception of values until we will it to be our own and accept it as such. Bullshit.

Internal position essentially differentiated by the formula

bottled up in solitary confinement. Commercials spilling affirmation of your right not to do anything with your biological development while polls police your attitudinal energy in longitudinal efficiency. You are not for THIS so therefore I am. Worth so much. Capable of spending. NOT FOR THIS. For that. And that and that and that too. We would be proud to know that you too are not for or not against depending on recent USA conglomeritization of the network. Marketplace where you sleep dreaming of forecasts showing predilection for upward movement of points charted on astronomically indebted shock and bondage big board scene. A vain attempt to interpret occasional volatility in the venal underworld of seats in the pit of hell. Field of delimitations places all value in centrifugal futility course networking its way toward an undetermined goal post? *Limit determinism* by cleansing the production crew once upon a time bomb. Plutonium. Triggers me to the final over-and-out big sleep.

Detonating delights delivered daily. Drudge duties deteriorate deranged dude's daring direction. One slip of the tongue and the Centralized Metaphors of Life

explode

send their cronies after you. Critical apparition sucks in reactive apparatus causing mild indigestion. Belly of sunshine rumbles in alkaline speed recovery. Reappropriates former role as big boss and mans the station. IN ALL SIX MILLION WERE BOUND BY LOVE. The ensuing skin to skin contact was so unavailable for comment that the regal forces continued to dream of coming muddy gunpowder on the faces of the unrest.

AMERIKA: GET OUT

(WHILE YOU STILL CAN)

THE TICKING
TIME BOMB OF HEAVEN

Narrative is Power. The interconnectedness of segmental being, no matter how inappropriate or falsely constructed, is the way we get turned on to the regiment of Power. Power deplores our usage of improvisation with mega jumpcut arbitrary free floating flotsam segueing into the dysfunctional sea. [With the aid of highly trained technicians in the field of action utilizing the channels of communication, we've been able to accomplish purposeful and scientific engineering of human subject matter.] Soul Brother, you dead. Future's in our hands now.

Even if my better self creatively investigates and acknowledges the right for narrative to implode and demarcate itself to the point of becoming an unrecognizable auto-fiction that doesn't portend any affiliation with the interconnectedness of segmental being, I might still find myself [or something creeping into my-*self*] openly engineering the power of conventional storytelling in such a way as to solidify my allegiance with a utopian death-wish for a world that, in the end, holds together. [The syntax might occasionally find itself smeared into the oblivion of a rootless grammatology now splitting the scene just as it gets what it supposedly wanted (sex, money, power, property, name recognition, etc.), but the overall effect of narrative no matter how transformative its content might be, is to create

devastatingly delicious Power, even if that Power leaves a
most bittersweet aftertaste in your awestruck mouth.] The
poetry of our time is a cancer eating itself away. A grey desert
whose muse is suffering from a catatonic contusion. I feel
dead.

But I am only spiritually dead. Physically I am alive. I seek out
and sensuously destroy the demarcated demeanor of every
young lass that has the guts to approach me. She'll approach
me right before a performance (if she can catch me) or she'll
tag along right after I'm finished letting my tirade of vocif-
erous vanity flood out of me in ways I can't describe here.
[The simple accommodation of being who she is and allowing herself to approximate my field of action by being here
with me as I sing my songs of delirious delusion is enough
incentive for me to butter her anal taxonomy so that I can
categorically ram her shit-encrusted imperatives just as they
feign a sense of style earmarked with the tidings of some soul
whose body begs for penetration. Even if one of us has AIDS
and knows it but doesn't bother telling the other about it,
we'll still be proud of our heritage, the one thing that keeps
us going: our Amerikan tradition: lying and/or deceitfulness.
Once you make that connection, anything, any dream, any
life whore-o-scope, any commercial power coming together
for the express purpose of legitimating the project's attempt
to ridicule the excesses of Power {illegible}…EVERYTHING
IS MORAL…]

Morally, I am free.

With this profusion of images bombarding the emotionally
depleted corruptible mass of ventilated flesh I call selfhood

(the body watching TV), the only recourse one has is to create units of energy so POWERFUL in their iconoclastic intensity that they blow the images away…[what sort of imagination could actually get away with even thinking such thoughts?]

I eat POWER. POWER eats me. POWER eating itself every-time I open my eyes, dream of the enterprise, Amerika, starship self exploring the lackluster universe in search of demonologies worthy of my critical eye, forever doped on the promise of commercial consent, the Everyday Man, WAKES UP, collides with the forces of chaos, creates a tenable gameplan full of sales assets benefits perks stream-lined segmentation of impossible fortunes wheeling and dealing in the glasnost roulette world of growth and merging if it'll let me?

It lets me.

Now what?

BAILOUT

Them hills over there sure do have some strange hombres. They beat their wives to bloody pulps. Collect the bloody pulp and pour it into the blender. Turn it on Liquify. Then they feed the fresh juice to their kids who grow abnormal big and strong. The boys take on the bodies of big ol' linebackers, the girls become tall, curvaceous co-eds who, once plucked then fucked, give birth to more boys and girls. As soon as they've rotted out their overmileaged wombs of activity, the men beat the shit out of them and put them in the blender.

These strange misogynists are part of a vicious cycle that many of us here in Happytown think'll never end. The big bad men who sock their women in the jaws and rip their hair and pry their legs open so as to force themselves into their ripened love-pits are really still the little boys they were before they drank the liquified version of their little girl Mothers. I imagine it must get real confusin' makin' out who's who. Everybody's mind is a squash casserole the color of beet juice. The mush that passes for brains ain't nothin' to sneeze over either; it's what these varmints get by on. Real terrifyin' stuff over there. They call the town Merry Ka.

Merry Ka is sittin' on top some of the finest soil in these parts. They can easily grow themselves some of the finest tastin' organic vegie matter this planet's capable of producin'. We here in Happytown would like to have some of it too. We'll pay big bucks for it. Money's no prob, amigo. We made quite a bit of good hard cash back in the late 20th century sellin' some repossessed property we done bought back from the government. Actually, the repossessed property used to be our property, property we bought with unconditional loans we rigged with our buddies sittin' on the boards of the best savings and loans institutions federally-insured money could buy. Feds actually had a reserve in them foolish days. Then the whole savings & loans thing went bust, we wuz partly responsible (although it was the guv who gave us the green light, they were the ones who rattled off the buzzword of the time, de-regulation was what they called it, we used to jokingly refer to it as nobody's-regulatin-it-so-you-better-grab-it-while-you-can, and so we did, and it was one big party for what seemed like the longest time, that's why we congregated here in the foothills and christened our home Happytown), but the feds, who still had a responsible role in dictatin' the happenstance surroundin' and permeatin' the economy, they realized after takin' it all away from us, that it just wasn't doin' 'em any good sittin' there collectin' dust, so, they kinda had no choice but to bring it to market where they'd auction it all off to whoever had the bucks to pay for it. Well, I'll tell ya, that just about blew us away, here we were 'bout shittin' in our pants cuz we thot for sure the feds wuz gonna lock us all up and throw away the key but then we realized since it was they who put the whole thing in motion by de-regulatin' the entire industry, that, well, let's just say that they owed us. So all the talk 'bout criminal activity that everybody tried to make sound so bad with threats of life imprisonment and whatnot, all that was really just a practical stance for the politicians and businessmen to take. It looked good. Made a real nice sound bite just around dinner time.

Naturally, we all in Happytown had all the bucks we needed. That's why we wuz happy. We dint worry none cuz the money wuz ours to keep. We had it stashed. It was in real safekeepin'. So that when the auctioneer came to town and asked if anybody had any money to bail the guv out and would anybody be innerested in buyin' up some of this cheap yet valuable property, well, we all knew the feds was playin' us straight, so we bought everything we had given to them due to default (it looked like they wuz forced to confiscate it all but really it was always theirs to possess, we just use the stuff as markers to play the game, don't matter here who really has a hold of it, the scorecard is moolah and we had so much of that stashed away we already and always knew who had won the only game that mattered, it was us, the pleasant folks of Happytown). So now we had all the money and all the property and needed us some good organic produce to keep us alive. Them folks in Merry Ka were xenophobic and didn't want nuthin to do with us.

We figger that purdy soon they'll be gettin' a taste for some of these here stagflated greenbacks. It's bound to happen. Man's gotta have his share of good hard cash. They can't hold out forever. We live in a takeover world, hostile takeovers, that's the reality. They know it we know it it's a known thing. They know they'll give in. They's just waitin' for the right time to do it. They so fuckin' stupid anyway. Beet juice wives, always a kid.

50 WAYS TO
MARKET YOUR LOVER

1. Word of mouth
2. Stream of consciousness
3. Advertising
4. desecrating previous generations of experience
5. making monumental claims about your current world perspective
6. segue into the next number without really trying
7. acting as if you never cared about any of this
8. slave auction
9. TV talk show hype
10. public radio / college circuit / underground network?
11. charting official and unofficial policy decision-makers' daily agendas
12. offer sales incentives guaranteeing major feedback from "dupe"
13. create Master then reprogram entire personage through effects processing
14. deprive glutinous mass of sexual fulfillment then rail them with totalitarian energy cleverly disguised in the rhetoric of a multi-national television broadcast coming into your home via superstate-implanted speakers that blast the words **YOU MUST OBEY**
15. Retail experience at a discount rate via simulation or a downgraded version of the empirical method
16. siphon off the energy apparently there although some-

times not so sure what it is I'm trying to say but am saying it anyways

17. create a newsletter that instructs your workforce on how to buy / prosper / meet expectations & get the most out of life without giving them enough **real cash dollars** to retire at an early age

18. if you retire at a young age and are therefore unproductive (not producing goods and services all in the name of God or GNP, same thing), then obviously you're a flailing pervert who's only interested in wild lustful enjoyable sexual activity and MUST BE ARRESTED so that you can no longer have any effect whatsoever on the cosmic consciousness' desire to experience the ultimate in high-tech body ejaculation

19. Marta was not alone. She had me. We were very much in love and knew what we wanted out of life. To be together. They separated us back in 1998. I was in confinement at some closed down military base somewhere in the Midwest (nobody knew exactly where). I had been busted for smoking a joint in my own home. I used to think that I was just overly paranoid and that things were probably better than my head would otherwise think. Now all I have time to do is think. I think as I cook the grub for all the other love-starved addicts of pleasure who were jury-rigged into a life of isolation.

20. marketing my lover is going into small business which the feds frown upon because that means there's more activity they have to control and eventually buy by-way-of their corporate cronies whose estates are really very beautiful and definitely worth slaving around in.

21. selling myself as my own lover is something I've often thought of doing although finding highly-reputable

would-be early investors of my product line isn't as easy as I thought it'd be   it seems as though I'm too eccentric

22. But time has a way of catching up with history-in-the-making and maybe my innate knowledge of the business ledger will afford me the opportunity to create the greatest subsidiary the oligarchy has ever had time to consider its friend

23. building a list of possible sources of interest, people who will jump on your lover's bandwagon, will take a lot of time and effort

24. try cable TV

25. your local library

26. on the pedestrian mall, take off your clothes, rupture

27. "be" SOMEBODY SPECIAL (on TV)

28. videocassettes (self-help, promo, simulated blowjob, ex-wife tells all)

29. National Public Radio special feature on your ability to

30. friends talking, lots of friends, talking, make friends

31. package: book, CD, audiocassette (talking-book), record, computer disk, movie, music video, party, world tour, simulcast (teleconference a "happening", YOU)

32. seem like you're not interested in any of this and that it's a waste of time and counterproductive and then when somebody you know does it very successfully, cut them down for selling out (do this on TV, preferably cable)

33. go religious, change your name, amplify all feedback

34. create Master then reprogram mission directives through digital effects-processor

35. accept the mortal morsels stuck in between your teeth and only when the time is right FLOSS (timing is EVERY THING: are you too early? are you too late? are you just right? who decides?)

36. consider participating in benefit performances that will substantiate your desire and/or willingness to reach out and touch the people in a real genteel way (be human)

37. assume the body (individual) is naturally reckless and nervous when forcibly controlled in The Land of Political Bodies and let the muscles twitch for a brand new switch (Siouxsie and the Banshees)

38. the reasonable man adapts to the world; the unreasonable man persists in trying to adapt the world to himself. Therefore all progress depends on the unreasonable man (that's George Bernard Shaw, thanks George, and let's not forget about reasonable women, the ones who **know** that the shit has hit the fan, that the balance of terms isn't a balance but rather a lopsided landslide of rigged hegemony persisting in our collective memory!)

39. create extravagant experiments (for example, transgress your individual body's private-pleasure mode by assuming the disposition of the political body as if it **were** the personal prose you found yourself becoming, then, poeticize the moment of your "becoming" by going nationwide on cable TV)

40. the lover is bliss reincarnated as an industrial waste product coming to you live via satellite, your heart is burning, gas?

41. chocolate cream-filled truffles fill your mouth as she enters more accessible data into the terminally-ill base of operations

42. depress the mechanism and the social unrest begins

43. coverage of the revolution is spontaneously transmitted to our affiliates in Tokyo, Bonn, Berlin, Kyoto, Frankfurt, Kobe, Munich, Hiroshima

44. Marta makes me mad. Me masticate Marta. Marta mimics

me, masticates, mimics me more. My Marta markets me. Masticates my me mightily. Makes me Marta. Marks me Marta. Mine.

45. Can I have your attention please?
46. Tonight's performance has been preempted. The cursory device has lost its syntagm and all personnel are needed to cover (up the sickness).
47. Thank you
48. Thank you
49. Thank you
50. Thank you

SILENCE AGAINST ITSELF, OR
DO "I" KNOW HOW TO READ "ME"?

WE HAVE BEEN NOTIFIED that your Signifying Other dripping nightsleep in perpetual dreamrotation is hereby acknowledging the right for you and others to use and/or reproduce the slide-effective sub-ridiculouso virtuoso played by Dick Reader Senior Transaction Analyst at Bank Unification home of the ministry mystery hour and corporate flower power.

Child psychoanalysis inclined to lay the laconic stratagem of neologistical nightmares creating warfare pact with middle eastern peace patrol units dangerously appealing to the business cycle mind in monthly fee losing quark capability available at bookstores near jews.

Hot dude wet alignment drumming up support for the programs and services offered by Direct Sperm Flotation R.E.M. synchronicity somehow opening quality laboratory of rat manifestation overexposed to the crack addict's asshole pouring out of its own skull fucking skeletal scream job.

Terrorist forces send uzi shivers through K-Mart cashier's window of opportunity until the process withdraws into itself and becomes nothing but the chemical additive cleverly ingrained into the collective consciousness' serene nonidentity.

Dick Reader seeing the fall of phallogocentric subjectivism while the punning pupa with its green hair on fire lights a joint smokes a guitar and belches out a lyric sending derelict demagoguery guaranteed to create soliloquies composed of are you experienced vinyl matters.

When approaching Dick Reader who is not a hemorrhoid condition and willfully dismembers him/herself from the company of "It" as "It" develops into a sequestered programs and services operational unity scheme to further malfunction the uppity undergrowth perilously sticking its head out from underneath the surface completes itself but only for a millisecond that can't even be read by the naked eye so you tell me if it's worth it.

Restorative vocabulary of the vanquished Men who once not too long ago had Time to handle their amorous transgressions but now formulate a new improved Space Technology to do all their dirty work for them (close-up of live seaweed swirling around her neck softly massaging her pent-up energy coated in a cryptic passage of orgonometric psychosynthesis).

Demented Dick Reader's silent night of fructose seeping out from underneath his/her skinnydipping Eden experience of dew drops and doe dips into the hypersurreal crucial metastasis jiggling warm obesity right under his/her nose.

Day in the life of Cig Fried coach potato cooking up a storm of brewing ideas passing himself off as an i.d. in the making or an Id for the taking is her idea of a good time rock and roll encyclopedia of endless opportunity exposing itself to the careertracking mind of TV's next generation of mutant memorabilia.

Northeast cool shuffled together with an endless indian summer's shot in the Rocky Mountain dark dreaming its way to the West Coast where the ideas get transformed some three hours later OUR TIME (the plight of Amerika going nowhere really fast). OUR TIME has come. The manic throwing together of whatever you are is now out in the OPEN. Survival of the fittest all the swivel chairs lubricated with entry level cum juice fortified with vitamin sleaze. The rich fiber optic network's colon cancer dripping an excess worth mentioning insofar as GNP is concerned (::::::::::::: really ::: gross ::: national ::: poop ::: standard / who secretly scoops?). Dick Reader's communication with the unknown. Metaphonetic beauty in ecstasy. Interpolation seduced by the thought of instantaneous orgasm. An impossible moment of savage energy absorbed in the composition of freeform autoeroticism passing through every other cell of energy the universe creates.

MULTIPLE CHOICE

1. Every Good Standard Deserves a Reconciliation
   a) running ramrod truck filled with Burts and Big Sams
   b) all the lying feces telling stories in a shit bar
   c) emphasis on growth potential as it mediates your spiltshift life
   d) answering machines bestowing voices awkward in love

2. The Ever-Expanding Self Fadded Out On Advertisment Hype
   a) right wing extremist categorical genius strung out norm
   b) everything tastes better with bluebonnet on it
   c) melt away the heartache melt away the tears
   d) going down on love lost in the scream of a squall

3. Lying Dead in the Regent Cafe
   a) money for nothing chicks for free
   b) bloated ego deflated by deconstructive freshman from Kansas
   c) I came I shattered I traversed I went
   d) Thanks for the memories (Hopeless)

4. Essay in Utilitarian Existentialism
   a) curtains crawling up the wall infinitely attracted by bugs

b) no return to ancient rock glitter crystalized in Mr. Meth
c) Tommygun Hairspeed roaming the campus looking for pleasure victims
d) I came I saw I did it I faltered I eventually fucked I went

5. Clubbing It With Weird Capitalist Connoisseur of Crap Commodities
   a) "I met her the last time I was here...she only likes Black guys..."
   b) dressing for the occasion
   c) undressing for the liasion
   d) stripped to the bone/cellophane wrapper wear/love preserved

6. Darting Up The Stairs He came Upon Her Highness The Loot
   a) May I take this opportunity to introduce myself?
   b) I am the newest in WRITERMAN motifs struggling to subsist
   c) Here in the Vast Disregard of Regal Performance my flatulence asks
   d) The Princess wondering if I would participate in a urination free-for-all

7. He who used to play wordjazz over the airwaves in New York City is now
   a) disease-eaten brain mixing his metaphors
   b) some strange soul assuaging via manipulative neck maneuvers
   c) I came I really had a blast and I really left

    d) split the scene not knowing who I was for a moment but then

8. She finally accepted the fact that I was the Man for her
    a) arbitrarily making up a network of interconnected "beings"
    b) one of the people involved in the dilemma, a hustler named Crue
    c) we struggled into New Orleans with a beach on our backs barking
    d) eventually the ordeal subsided and the happy homemakers were

9. How This Came To Be or How I Drove Myself To Do It
    a) drinking espresso in the Regent Cafe talking New Age politics
    b) her highness The Loot overwhelming me with subtle discharge
    c) losing touch with workaday commodity-infested slave labor
    d) technocracy of her inner loin automatic juicer spraying lethal

10. Easier Dead Than Done
    a) Imagination persevering through it all even though blood guts
    b) wearing thin around the margins of the brain bearing mindcrack
    c) sometimes it feels as though this always ends up essaying
    d) recent influx of pop-rock craze rejuvenated 24-hour commercial

11. Her Highness makes up for lost time by expediting our case
    a) "Do you promise to honor respect inject and intuitively inaugurate?
    b) "wherever you are whatever you do always remember that vows
    c) "hanging in the a e i o u and sometimes wondering why"
    d) we cannot afford to quote ourselves anymore (we're dead)

12. The Force of The All-Mighty Dreamweaving Flamethrower is Now Here
    a) desires creeping into my field of limitations makes me open
    b) soon a whole shitload of feelings get expressed in strange brews
    c) radical chic apportionment misses me barely and I'm starving for
    d) anything REAL and FUNCTIONAL in an obscuritan love code

13. The Puritan Inside Me Makes Its Way Out Into Her Soft Vagina Humming
    a) already I'm beginning to barter my body away
    b) conveniently falling in love only to forget the vowels that got me there
    c) spinning out meals of fortune with Vanna sunsets closing the mind
    d) deregulating the Institution so that my money's for nothing and

14. Claiming the right way to approach Freedom he spoke of Peace through
    a) too many times I've offered these options to you and only now
    b) every good Destroyer deserves a Major
    c) potential fuck-ups reenlisting so as to practice the fine art of
    d) see if you can find the highlights of World Warm Freeze III

15. Hoping to derive copasetic pleasure from wheeling and dealing in tongues
    a) an expert marksman named Mark Man with voodoo mohawk hairspeed
    b) ranging on the homefront carrying on a tradition of nihilism railing
    c) how many loose problematics does it take to disinvest in
    d) perhaps we should acknowledge the fact that were we to be

16. Meatpackers memorializing the futurekind of kindred spirits
    a) splattered across the cafe table that's where it comes together
    b) CIA terrorist bombings in San Fran year 1995
    c) foreign agents displacing local Heads via remote control
    d) caught in the triangulation strangulation of Them Us We

17. Final Propositions Finding Their Way Out Of This Mess
    a) she came she saw it she took it she blew it she ate it she split
    b) emptyheaded drinking more decaf espresso in hopes of attaining
    c) wondering if the newsprint would carry cover coerce coincide
    d) It has nothing to do with the story now in the process of becoming

18. Mr. Meth never snorted anything out of the blue
    a) detergent bleach grease remover happily tranquil people polling
    b) tap water sandwiching mind against poison producing new age deli warfare
    c) combat zone of internal necessity forming nuke angst creaming
    d) deregulating urinating knowing unknowing becoming disappearing

19. Whenever you sense The End Is Nearing always remember to
    a) examine the procedures used thus far and see if the quest
    b) if by chance the vocal capacity of the singer seems to be
    c) or abide by the electric guitar influence of Hendrix or
    d) so that no matter who you are and where you see this you'll always

20. Time to eat lunch and go for a hike in the mountains
    a) the writer totally sexed generative flux melting
       wishes to
    b) if you have any questions regarding the voice inside
       the text please
    c) leave a message on my answering machine and I'll
       be sure to
    d) forming cellular loops out of trashed fiber optics I
       found in the

CHANNELING VISION

I'm not ALL FOR total NONSENSE but then again I'm not totally
AGAINST

I'm not totally against all fours being pronounouns nor am I
definitively excised from the complete unexpurgated ROCK N ROLL

if you feel the total foul-up FOR all things MEANINGFUL is somehow
antagonistic to your otherwise Pronominal Being There Always then

try out lukewarm reception of not-so-sure-of-themselves eyes
masquerading as tainted young upstarts rallying behind a flag of

NOTHING in its right mind would ever wander into the precipitous
regional gunsling of quick-draw happenstance whereby the those

IN THE KNOW totally for ALL meaning redundant reading apparatus
filling the need of some social welt forming fast on its ASS

corporeal indignity climbing up the ladder of SUCKING SEX while
rebelling without helter-skelter mind movements over the page

STILL WATER strumming nonexistent poetic along the breeze of
out of tune alumni agents prescribing reading assignments for

INDIVIDUALS for the AGAINST MODE of reproduction because who can tell if she'll really wench out and dawdle to your open-eyed

CATASTROPHEapostropheprepossessingtheindignantPronounouns
who go oui oui in the night

wetting the bed with Formal nocturnal emissions that go oui oui
in the night

the night

selling bodily parts at an incredible discount first the bottom
of her feet the so-called soles of her meager existence then

selling off large bunches of her hair blond straw grass strewn
haystacks flown over the frenzied fire

IT ALL MAKES SENSE

sucking her clit until it runs dry only it never runs dry and then
out of nowhere you find yourself incapable of coming up for air

and so you die

and that's your story

and it was boring

but no one ever told you how it all was supposed

but that's okay too because in this day and AIDS

drowning in it seems so precious

precious and pink
            precious and pink and perhaps

from the other end
of the spectrum you get

            but where was she coming from?

that's okay too
you can always leave out the details or if you wish
insert some made-up glob of gook to help debunk her
Caretaker

Caretakers er er er er er er
working in their plots
menstruating blood clots
and enriching the soil

somehow this all seems toiled
toyed out

boy oh boy wouldn't an other-guy other-style WRITERMAN be just
the thing to set this baby in motion!   oh well   mean-o-pause
                        struthead going
                        nowhere ::: lost
                            in
                                the
                            hotflash
                            that makes
                                me
                            wanna
                            shout!

but he doesn't shout.
instead: he shits.
gotta shit   you know that.
drink coffee   write prose
take shits.   This is what
writers do.   Isn't it?
Ever try drinking coffee
in order to get the im
agination rolling only
to find that you can't
finish your sentences
because you gotta run
to the toilet to take
a shit? And then you
make it back to the
page and the momentum
's gone   the whole
thing disintegrated!
evaporated! poof!

that's why I now have a raised commode
as a writing chair ::: this way I can
write and drink coffee *and* shit
all at the same time. Fiction will never be the same again. It'll be
the real shit. The only shit worth taking. All the rest'll be
inauthentic synthetic inundated imm imm imm imm imm immi grant?

Emma Loo.

Emma Loo drew figures.
Her own included.
One of me with her body wrapped closely around me.

Gum paper.
Awx

that's wax.

That's technology apparently

so if you feel the need to write back and want to discover what
kind of person you are when you get around me then Imm imm immm
imm imm imm   but remember   no negatory   only
small love birds with comedrops glistening on their wings

only feathery freaks fucking up a surrealistic pillowtalk

going oui oui in the night

the night

this portion of the broadcast has been declared excerpted from

this portion of the broadcast has been declared a blighted area

this portion of the broadcast is now under federal regulations

this portion of the broadcast is currently unable to

this portion of the broadcast is under the direct supervision of

this portion of the broadcast is not really happening

this portion of the broadcast is a good place to reel in your only other

this portion of the broadcast is reaching more than

this portion of the broadcast is officially affiliated with or sponsored by

this portion of the broadcast is coming to a close

this portion of the broadcast is tempering blue skies forever

this is a test   for the next 289 years your monitors will be put

ON HOLD

AMERIKA AT WAR:
THE MINI-SERIES

THE VISION THING

Clean slate. Promiscuous sleight of hand slinging wordburgers on a grill billed as the best in the biz. Who is the prognosticator of all this retromilitarism? Rehash & Headstash. General Psyche and his sidekick Major Uptight. Liquid dysfunctionalism. The Tube In All Her Glory ("Please leave out all the gory details, we got children watching this fatal attraction...").

Follow the (film) leader. Video bombardment. So much gameshow talk with added color by White Supremacy (of the male kind). Kindred spirits evoke Superbowl mentality as rookie wide receiver catches the latest smart bomb in the end-of-all-Time zones. One Ubiquitous Nation, under God, intercepting scud missiles (allah god's children running for cover) lost in Anal Contraction Zones. CNNtrol effect introduces itself immediately there's no time for delay this is the hottest story since I last got taken over (by a very public company : The U S of A-holes).

Wrote a poem just now. It went

TV's simulation
canon fodder
war groupies
dressed in silk Amerikan flags
sucking off the sum total of commercialism in formation ...

As if to say

AMERIKA : THIS SCUD'S FOR YOU ! ! !

THE BRIEFING

The briefing came across as a mad brothel scene with military men demanding submissiveness from everyone attending. Four-star General Psyche was saying "I'll take the one with long blond hair and electromagnetic horsesucking capability," while his sidekick, Major Uptight, was asserting his desire for the cute Southern Belle masquerading as an Airman who once thought that military might equaled education/money/security/decent standard of living/a future.

The windblown residue of sand and sperm and anointed womanly cum blew throughout the night while an unlimited array of preordained orgies camouflaged themselves as sorties. There were gorgeous power jobs fabricating the farce beyond recognition. Righteousness permeating unlimited fields of operation creaming me. Amerikan might. My come.

"That's all we have for you now. Go get some sleep. Turn off your projectors and let the silence begin."

There was always the AIDS factor. If you were unable to make do on out-of-commission artillery tanks or the occasional mirage of selfsustained Amerikan sexorgans, then you could always expose yourself to the enemy and demand that HE (the immoral creep with a payload of destruction) cram his bacteriological missile-dickhead into your hot steamy chemsuit. You could beat your breast in the midday sun and yell "I'm an Amerikan, I'm here to preserve my lifestyle, I'm on the side of everything good, I'm blowing your fucking brains out …" And if that didn't work, you could always write all wrongs away by composing real-time poetry campaigns that our satellite divisions back in the "free" West would try to suppress with all their egocentric might. Your poem would read

> *Just slumming, me*
> *a mindset fortification*
> *goal stomping end zones*
> *segregated dreams*
> *here in The Middle East*
> *(my wartime ghetto)*

CONSUMER BULLETS

Artillery The Hun, plainclothes officer of the Amerikan embodiment, pulled out all the stops. His chief weapon was chemical, man, like total napalm destruction. Like this dude was bad, man, real bad, like he was the next Hitler. Like he was Agent Orange on the loose ready to goose you with his searing chem warhead.

He was not good looking. Not as good looking as the NBC reporter in Saudi Arabia. In fact, 96% of the women polled in Amerika, said they'd rather NOT sleep with the enemy. (This, in stark contrast to the invasion of Libya, where a whopping 86% of the women polled admitted an odd kind of animal magnetism toward the curly haired Kaddafi). So much for Fatal Attractions.

Only fags burn flags?

The more you support the murder the more you cleanse yourself of it.

One enemy civilian casualty can be successfully erased by buying two boxes of Cheer detergent. That's right, buy two, erase one! Now is the time for all good countrymen to buy two of everything. To double up. Buying Power equals

Confidence. Confidence equals Growth. Growth is Anti-Recessionary. Anti-Recessionary activity proves that War, though not what we want, is still, in its own way, Good. All Good Countrymen. All Pretty Consumers...lined up in a row. So much to choose from and so very little time! Geez: I can't decide. Does anybody *want* to be the next Amerika?

Reconnaissance Flyer meets Renaissance Man.

Flying overhead, RF sees RM working the keyboard at speeds so fast that RF feels he must inform RM that what he's doing is detrimental to the nation's health.

RM claims that what he's doing is exercising his right to Free Expression.

RF informs RM that Free Expression is an oxymoron.

RM queries as to who the real moron really is.

RF drops his payload of obliteration over RM's headquarters (his home).

The news reports come in claiming that "collateral damage" is still being assessed.

RF is interviewed after the game while Senators whose faces are in ruin pour champagne over his beaming with pride Head.

One reporter wants to know what RM looks like from way up in the sky.

RF says (in his most charming electrifying photogenic manner) that he looks like a scurrying flea on the back of a wheezing homeless person.

Pats on the back from all the Senators/followed by a car commercial.

sortie

      party

sortie

      party

sortie

      party

sortie

      party

    sortie

        party

    sortie

        party

          e

            x

              p

                l

                  o

                    d

                      e

                        s!!!!!!!!!!!!!!!!!!!!!!!!!!

                      H O U S E

                      f   n

                            e

                            m

                            y

          bodies of

          the dead

          buried in

          their own

          rubble

carrying around
your package of "difference"
what once might've been a blur of indistinctiveness
(culture, counterculture / aesthetic, anti-aesthetic)
now is Black & White
with minor patches of grey matter that are in the process
of separating (don't mix with colors, ALWAYS USE BLEACH)

nothing of imaginative significance really happening

the complicitous voice of the multinational/military/media
                              MOUTHPIECE
                    (let's call it

                                        3M)

the voice of 3M
telling you the story the way THEY want it to be told
(non-narrative yes, commercial-free no)
for example, War

the ultimate consumer item

(buy one while it lasts!)

                    the question being:
            where does the writer/artist fit into all this?
        would celebrating the bureaucratic consumer society's
            logo-slogan mentality insure the writer/artist
            his or her place in the mega-cash jackpot of
                        crony operations?

the voice of 3M
invites YOU (as reader/writer/artist/critic)
to take part in this landslide victory
of language divorced from meaning!

come join in the fun
and reap all the benefits!!

> support
> yourself
> as THEIR self
> so as to
> support yourself
> as an artist?

CAN'T BE DONE

he(or)she who plays up to the media oligarchy
spilling their individuality in floods of I'm-one-of-you-too
economic voodooism

> (is making money via writing surviving or
> is writing itself, the creative act, survival?
> who's fueling who?)

> shall be called "collaborator"

he(or)she who sees fit to disrupt the dyseased culture's
(meta)physical violence on/against the creative self
who'll perform acts of anti-aesthetic terrorism
with language & technology & love & freeform desire
networking its way into the imaginations of those
whose gates are OPEN

shall be called "resister"

REGISTER NOW ! ! !

CREATE YOUR OWN SELF ! ! !

TRANSPOSE YOUR LOVE ON THE WORLD'S ABOMINABLE CANVAS ! ! !

SING THE BODY'S PLEASURE
INTO DEEP DARK HOT SLEEP ! ! !

cher love,

i'm just becoming aware of my prejudice against the
proclamation of anything new. new writing, new music,
new world order. the folks who brought us the most
recent TV hit, *Amerika At War: The Mini-Series*, are now
really truly once and for all taking the avant-garde stance
back from artists. despite its disloyalty to the term itself
(the death machine is not ahead of anything), we still
have to admit that the militaristic mongrels on the march
INTO THE TWENTY-FIRST CENTURY are, in fact, the
leaders of a NEW WORLD ORDER. i may sound as though
i'm contradicting myself but that's because "contradic-
tion" & "ambiguity" & all such manner of hit and misin-
formation are the conditions we live under. & i mean
under. i've never felt so taken over in all my young life.
lying is the standard. The IN THING is vision, a vision
uncluttered / unpolluted by the heartfelt tragedy of
(bloody) events. Vision is TECHNOLOGY so sure of itself
that it doesn't have time to pee (or shit or fart or screw or
drink a beer). Vision is a MAN who no longer SEES & then
INTERPRETS, rather, it's a STAND-UP LEADER (i'm not
going to call him comic because i don't think it's funny at
all) who TELLS the person TUNING IN exactly what is
HAPPENING. & what if this TELLING is nothing but an
ADVERTISEMENT for the TELLERS THEMSELVES? well,
what else, cher love, you either buy into it or you stay put
(you better shut up & NOT SAY ANYTHING in opposition
to this ONE WAY OF TELLING or THE WORLD [the
uniform vision being created for your express understand-
ing] will unite against you). the hidden despotism of the
censorial ilk is just now reloading its bombs with ink.

151

psyche on the blink. no time to think. gotta go.

your one true amerikan cadet suffering from uni-sortie
overload

bloodless
human
shields
fielding
questions
answering
bombs
precision
pinpoint
destruction

columns surface
of to
disgust air
ruins enlightenment
on feeling
parade happy
infant to
mortality be
rate alive
in making
combat money
zone creating you
filtering Time yours
technological victorious youth
imagination animal young
untouched pounding yourself
democracy hairy yowling?
races chest
unfettered in
speeds defiance
unencumbered of
TOUCHDOWN oblique

reference
to
death
machine
with
Presidential
dummy
ventriloquist
talking
out
both
sides
of
ITS
mouth

i wondered
why there
was so
much open
space in
my wartime
writing &
i realized
that there
are all
these GAPS
that never
get filled
open holes
childhood wounds
insufferable guilt
superego needs
lodged inside
mass consciousness'
unyielding hate
campaign against
itself

this
is
the
space
we
destroy

the
desert
of
our
souls

the
place
where
we
kill
our
fear
of
death

```
TTTTTTTTTTTTTTTTTTTTTTTTTTTTTTTTTTTTTTTTTTTTTT
T
T
T
T                       V
T                       V
T                       V ictory
T                       V
T                       V
T
T
T
T
T
TTTTTTTTTTTTTTTTTTTTTTTTTTTTTTTTTTTTTTTTTTTTTT
```

OUR & WE

language: ultimate strategy: get the lingo: then turn on
the jingo

spectacle: turn on the vid: then ransack the id: moral
fabric designed by latent homosexual huckster who
secretly pays off Congressman to NOT vote FOR new AIDS
allocation bill

heterosexual mist: cloudy transfiguration of thought
rising inside his pants: meanwhile she incorporates her
one-act play of disgust as the centerpiece to her militant
feminist artperformance and gets banned from the
airwaves: His Majesty the King of Nukes doesn't like *that*
kind of jingoism on his TV/radio stations: what are we
fighting for (she asks this as she pours hot velveeta cheese
over her tattooed naked body): just ask the network
anchordroid: it'll tell you: it's one word: FREEDOM

our way of life: the way we do things here: the priorities:
how can our artists who suffer the economic military
political woes of harried hegemony NOT spill tears of
indictment all over the streets of our dead cities?: the

moral bombast twisting lingo into softcore missile porn
blowing its own horn hiding its itinerant horniness (all
the soldiers say they can't wait till it's over / they want to
go home): who do the generals in the desert fuck?: their
camels?: i'd rather walk a hundred miles than fuck a
camel: the metaphoricity of humping (dry humping) is
only a camel away: oasis of pleasure to-be-found in the
moral/money/megadeath machine complex of Reason &
oversimplified inarticulation

our men & women are doing it in the sand: we have to
continue our support for what is ours: what's ours is ours
and what's theirs is ours because we know what's right:
we know what's good: our consciences tell us that what
we do in the name of good is right & true & bold & worth
it: always: always: always: **we** know **ours** is to have and
to hold and to protect: don't fuck with us: don't mess
with **ours**: **we** in the desert: **we** be the ones: **we** be the
ones who die for them: who them?: turn on the TV and
find out: they ain't ashamed to show they face: they got
us support: they say we: they say ours: they say us: **we**
deliver on command

MALDOROR SINGS THE PRAISES OF VICTORY
(or sorties of glory camouflage whatever's gory)

Touchdown ! !
Touchdown ! !
The Eagle Has Landed ! !
Amerika's scored again ! !
An incredible victory ! !
What a wipe-out ! !
What a massacre ! !
WHAT A FUCKING KILLING MACHINE WE GOT GOING FOR US ! !

back to you Peter
back to you Dan
back to you Tom

Tom/Peter/Dan
(as One, as Usual):   Thanks Mark. Wow. Incredible. An-
                           other killer Amerikan victory. When
                           will it ever end? Who can stop us
                           now? I think we're gonna go all the
                           way. There's just nobody out there
                           capable of stopping us. The Russians
                           are having an awful season, their
                           whole team appears to be in a man-
                           agement crisis. The Germans are
                           banned from activity due to their
                           previous recruiting violations. The
                           French are barely able to put together
                           a team. There's really nobody out
                           there. What do you think, John, la-

dies and gentlemen, our senior advisor, color commentator, John Minister.

John: You're right Tom. There's really no one out there. It's been a devastating kill from the start. The enemy hasn't been in it from the opening sortie. Where's their defense? Their offense? I don't know what their leaders could've been thinking. This is a slaughter, true & bold.

AGIT PROP STOP GAP

(field report by Mark Amerika, Agit Prop Coordinator, Fiction Ink)

This disease I found myself becoming, an Amerikan, true and bold, was running out of control, rampant on the scene of our mutual disgust, and I loved it, it was a feeding ground for everybody who knew that to live was nothing more than losing their creative selves to the artificial means of production whose disposal was YOU, you who wake up in the morning and bring yourself to the cumulative psyche of Amerika, the garbage disposal, the streets of your cities deterritorialized by capital terrorism, the contamination filtering through your body so that the language you spew forth becomes a random assortment of criminal sales tactics designed to reregulate the person you come into contact with's sense of self...as if such a thing as a self could still exist...

How can it? For the pleasure-seeking Amerikan self who desires nothing but complete insatiation, the chance to prolong the final orgasm that scares the shit out of its rudimentary think-nothing-of-it mind, there's only one mode of production, and that's the one that's given to each individual at birth, each birth tragic in that it never resolves its perennial dilemma, that of the flesh and its needs, until death, and Amerika doesn't want to know about death, because death doesn't deceive and if Amerika is anything it's a national consciousness geared toward deception, willful deception, the ultimate state of lying (to oneself), of turning imminent disaster into a superficial cry for freedom, a special brand of Amerikan freedom that secures all of ones idiosyn-

cratic insecurities, the feelings that never find consumma-
tion, the desires that regurgitate in the mixed mass media of
commercial consciousness…commercialism, not capitalism,
is what makes Amerika, the whore nation, take its licks so as
to keep on ticking. Time is the material that Amerika enslaves
your mind with. What we need is a new Amerika. What we
need is Timelessness.

A roundtable discussion by some of this nation's leading news correspondents and military experts has been going on for almost two hours. Let's sneak in here at the end and see how they wrap it up:

David Newman: I'm pleasantly surprised at how well we've managed to tear the hell out of their offensive capability. We're the most powerful nation on earth. We protect Freedom the whole world over.

Burt Reason: I think David is right. There's no two ways about it. There's one nation here on earth, one that matters, and that's the one that goes where it wants to go and reams the bad guys out of this unpredictable world. You know, sometimes we speak of our nation under God, well, I have reason to believe that as a nation we *are* God. We're not *under* anybody now.

Tammy Verb: Assuming that the war goes on longer than expected, do you think that the dissent in this country…

Max Pollster: …there IS no dissent in this country. I haven't seen any and I, like everybody else, have been totally tuned in to what's happening. And there's no way we're gonna see this thing go on any longer than it has to. Most

Amerikans, able to come home from a long abusive day at work, know that the men and women in the gulf are fighting for their way of life. They know that, for example, without this necessary evil, this hyperrealistic dreamtrip of wartime coverage, they would, perhaps, forget how lucky they are to be able to plop on couches thousands of miles away from the battlefield, which, by the way, the majority of people polled no longer see as a battlefield. 64% of Amerikans polled said they viewed the Big Picture as a computer-generated gameboard of operations. 94% of those polled said that they'd be PROUD to help key in whatever was necessary to insure us victory. Victory is what our economy needs right now. Consumer confidence before the war was spiraling downward at a pace not seen since the Great you-know-what. So really it's victory at any cost. We've gotten used to the fact that Amerikans no longer create valuable goods and services in the name of quality-of-life. We've got other dreamnations to do that for us. We create Debt. Debt is WHO WE ARE. Debt is WHAT WE LIVE FOR. The creation of debt is what turns us on, this is how we get off…[almost out of breath, a deep panting with drivel dribbling down his double-chin…]

David Newman: And not just the creation of debt or the simulated version of war, but the ability to eventuate it all in the Super Bowl of dreams, our national heritage…

Burt Reason: And not just the Super Bowl of dreams, but the commercials too, you know, "we here at the Texaco Corporation want to take a minute to thank the troops for all they're doing for us…" *It really is our way of life!*

Tammy Verb: Be all you can be ! ! (or not to be, that is the challenge!)

Burt Reason: Yes, and we'll have a helluva party when you get home!

Max Pollster: I think we needed this war. I haven't felt this good since World War Two.

David Newman: Don't forget Saddam Hussein. The surreptitious catalyst.

Tammy Verb: Yes, Saddam's a madman. Saddam and madman are almost anagrammatical.

Burt Reason: Oh well, *almost* doesn't count except in horseshoes and hand grenades.

Max Pollster: *And* nuclear weapons...

[all the panelists laugh at that last one, some uncontrollably, as the camera dollies back into another space]

Valentine's Day?

Dear Buried Control,

I just remembered that it's not V-Day at all but President's
Day!
Another great Agit Prop Stop Gap scenario ! !
MOM!   DAD!   I'm NOT coming home!!

Yours forever,
Rosebud

(Kane,
wake up,
the party's over,
Kane,
get up,
it's time to take over another country,
c'mon Man, get up, we gotta
take over this country. Don't
die on me now, not in my prime,
we gotta go in Man, we gotta
Occupy, like Bigtime Money Hustle,
like we oily birds catchin the germ.
We got that high-flyin flag-wavin
germ fluid happening Bigtime bro.
Get up ! ! We got The Vision Thing.
We got The New World Order.)

the liquid dementia evaporating in the mist of their portable love-confusion a series of roundtable talks about their mutually cornered future activity SPEWING FORTH A RANDOM ASSORTMENT OF CRIMINAL SALES TACTICS "always in quotes especially from a Pentagon or White House spokesman" we already know that what we're reading here is cleared by the military even if General Psyche & his comrade in suppression Major Uptight never but maybe they HAVE had a chance to see what it is I'm writing (he thought) maybe someone from "Intelligence" (it deserves quotes don't you think?) maybe a third-rate conservative ideologue who paid his professors to get Bs maybe that's who reads what I so willingly provoke & maybe he (or she) MAYBE A HE & A SHE (BOTH / TOGETHER) ARE WORKING ON MY PORTFOLIO it was Burroughs who said that a paranoid was someone who had all the

FACTS
AT HIS DISPOSAL

this toxic sludge of words that always embarrasses me why can't I ever just shut up like the commercial captains of consciousness ask me to?

it would be so wonderful to be able to just shut the fuck up and say nothing to never challenge the systemic collusion with big money wartime heroes

and their artful dodgers sinking in front of the media monopoly microphones mouthing this or that about what's good & what's bad & who's good for

a few aerial bombardments & who deserves the whole shenanigans the full nine yards the total complete destruction/obliteration the

unprecedented torment & upheaval the unrequited love the loony ego boost campaign with all collateral damage waived in lieu of pressing

opportunistic hype advertisements dropping their leaflets of pro-gun unitarian baptist holy war manifesto mini-series docudrama featuring

faces of the enemy who are just PEOPLE of the Wrong kind the Bad code the Mean spirit the Evil way the Cruel hoax the Necessary blood

this toxic sludge of post-industrial
waste is of nuclear unclear new
clear nuke lear knuckle under

uncle's blunder?

SAM WANTS YOU
(surface-to-air no more,
        now it's a quick
                tidy-up chore...

                life a bore?

                        well, then,

                                try WAR !

    it's easy
    it's quick
    it's clean
    it's entertaining!!!!

it's winning the ratings war!!!!!!!!!!!!!!!!!!!!!!!!!!!!!)

THE ENDS OF MAN

I. Freud (The Circumference of A Dream)

A.

She calls me on the phone and tells me she's dead. She says she's always been dead and that the loose luscious juicebag I've been sucking off of for the last five years is nothing but a figment of my imagination-lust-campaign-for-recognition. She tells me that she's the Ghost of Pussy Past and that as of this date I'm dead too although the true effects of this sudden departure won't be felt until I take the magic potion. I ask her what the magic potion is (I don't really want to know but that's my voice asking so now I anticipate her reply). She pauses exactly three minutes and thirty-three seconds without saying a word. I can't even hear her breathing. The word DEAD superimposes itself on my eyes while a rusty razor blade slashes disfigures liquidates whatever meaning my life may have had. "It" has returned.

B.

Now I'm in another world although I don't know how I got here. At first it's very hard to distinguish if I'm on the inside or the outside. The air is pink and the swollen lips that flap their fleshy wings all around me hum with an electric blue despair. It's a soothing drone and my body is lighter than light itself. Even as I feel the libidinous energy rush through my whole being I actually have no idea what this rush signifies or what this being procures. Just as I begin feeling the complete freedom of self-generated Spiritual Oneness, the intensity of the active dreammaking experience is somehow muddled by an enemy spokesman who assumes my every move is motivated by an uncharted sexual repression that fills all individuals who live within my national boundary. A linguisitic shot at philosophical delineation confuses the issue even more. All I know is that once again "I", corruptible mass of intemperate flesh, have become "It". An attempt to provide myself with a clear-cut understanding of what being "It" is all about now leaves me feeling empty and hopeless. Meanwhile the incessant rush of living sexcolour that supplies my every cell with boundless libido transforms me into a six-foot tall penis with a hairy head flagellating the ultra-sensitive layers of skin that surround me. The entire world I find myself lost in moans with pleasure and I realize that it's the giving of pleasure that satisfies my whole timeless essence. This realization causes me to completely lose track of myself and in that split second of total loss I find myself ejaculating the purest form of contamination the cosmos has ever produced. The payload is dropped off at the designated target zone. A white-hot explosion ensues and proceeds to annihilate any sense of identity I may have tried to potentialize during discharge. This sudden self-decontextualization causes the lips that surround me to scream. It's this screaming that wakes me up. I find myself in a bed that I've never been in before. The room is pink (just like my sister's). Aura is oral. My sex is being subtly obliterated.

II. Heidegger / Heisenberg / Wittgenstein

EGALITARIAN SOULSHIFT EMITS STRONG STENCH OF
LOVE AS MANY GERMS
AND THEIR SUPPOSED LOVED ONES RECONSTITUTE THE
VIGILANTE VIRUS
THAT DECOMPOSES THE LANGUAGE BLOCK AND TURNS
IT INTO JUICE

CONCENTRATED JUICE AMPLY LIQUIFIED AND SENT TO
THE CLEANERS FOR EVENTUAL WHITE-OUT ACKNOWL-
EDGES THE END OF MAN AND THE BEGINNING OF COLD
HYPERREAL SPACE FULL OF DYSFUNCTIONAL POETICS
APPLIED TO THE SCREEN MIMICKING DISASTER AS THE
ALL-TOO-HUMANE MONKEY MORTAL SQUEALS

meanwhile

First round draft choice date rapes Miss Genital Wart of 1993.
Plainclothes pimp officer playing punk music in jazz club
gets aced in his Whole and converts to New Age happiness.
Mark finds Fran doing her underwear and suggests
macrobiotics for dinner. Dave hides underneath a security
blanket of psychoactive fabric made especially for kids like
him. Is there an economic reason to help justify the fear

mentality pervading contemporary Amerikan sexuality? A
scientific reason? Psychological? Answer: Not too sure. But
let's blame the homeless. The homoerotics. The disenfran-
chised. The total lack of self-esteem?

Whatever it is, always remember to provide the one
thing that'll keep those meager paychecks coming: SERVICE
WITH A SMILE.
(service economy
S&M : service&memoryloss)

*********************time-for-a-commercial*********************

*Sirrrrrrrrrvice Enterprises proudly announces the arrival of their
new line of rambling robotics!!!!*
> *These remote-controlled agents of*
> temporary satiation promise you
> the best in automated genital licking!

Whoredom no longer has to be "human".
Even the vice-squad digs these creatures cuz they're LEGAL
THEY STIMULATE THE ECONOMY
> &
> ***they're happening!***

*Try (for example) Rodney Ruth, our latest greatest star performer.
Drafted from ROCKWELL UNIVERSITY INC., heshe'll suck yr
ballscunt off no prob no prob no prob!! And if you look inside
hisher's specially designed juicebag you'll see that our raspberry
flavored come is naturally colored with certified organic California*

beetjuice! The magic ingredients COME ALIVE IN YOUR MOUTH so that you have no choice but to swallow swallow swallow!! Taking it all in has never been so much fun!! Rodney Ruth is big black white creamy pink and delish! You can crank on this baby for as long as your mortality lasts!

Buy now and receive free of charge the 100% alloy "Big Ben" dildo attachment!

TIME IS ON YOUR SIDE!!

SATIATION GUARANTEED!!!!

(((((on the tube, during halftime, our president speaks:

> "Imagine the experience I had when I
> awoke to the sounds of Rodney Ruth
> *caught* in the act of auto-suck. It
> *literally* creamed me! It'll cream
> you too! The *perfect* weekend de-
> pository! Ages of intense warplay
> down the drain! But look at what
> we gain! It's INSANE!!"

extraterrestrial lipflesh invades my dreams again as I ponder the post-everything I always wanted out of Life's interplanetary environment / now I'm exploding the inmixing of all frayed genres as I lay myself beside the irreal horizon of

thorny flesh she so willfully supplies me with / a body coated
with sharp stinging clits each clit dabbed with the deadly
disease manufactured by ROCKWELL UNIVERSITY / and I
can't keep my tongue off her / "turn me on dead man, turn
me on dead man"

THESE THINGS HAPPEN.

WHY RELATIVITY?

WHY TURBULENCE?

III. Derrida / Foucault / Deleuze

Hi I'm Cheryl. Fuck me. Fuck you. I watch TV and yes in a way I kinda get off doing it (watching TV). TV is me screaming for attention. It's when I dig pretentiousness and when I begin to see the light. Any light. The fact is that I'm horny. I came here today to tell you I'm frustrated I'm angry I'm horny.

Please excuse my pumped up energy but I'm currently phasiiing in my recent extra iii face. My extra iii face has three eyes. It drips come and makes you wanna see the light too and I guarantee you that **you can see the light** all you have to do is send $19.95 we accept Visa Mastercard Amerikan Express. I love you.

The rest as they say is Herstory pumping so much come and shit and piss and fuck and cunt your way you don't know what to do with it all. It just drips out of my ears as I spontaneously erase what I create. A real whore of language. Can you dig?

My kids Zack and Zinka are ready to come your way. They're totally turned on to the idea of making it with someone older than them. They dig the sound of an old man coming a young girl coming a big mama coming a newness of ideology spreading its legs making oink moo buttfuck me sounds.

This is not even the end of it. They like to do all this with me. It's called child care. It's called deep-tissue meltdown. It's called CLOSE ENCOUNTERS OF THE THIRD REICH and it's spilling its guts out to you. Here I am. Here I come. Buttfuck me. I love you.

This is my friend Sheila. Sheila is a she-ra. She is ultra-tanned and has a baked off look. A baked off look is when you've strung out on UVs and are just in it for the fun. Kids on quaaludes sure she'll take it. Kids making creamcheese cake while high on grass sure she'll take it. Kids coming over to swim in her clitshaped pool sure she'll take it. **She'll take anything she can get her hands on!**

Centuries of swill

spilling up inside her side pain. Too much oxygen not enough oxygen. She must release. She must contort. She must reinvigorate. She is beautiful long brownred hair dripping out of my ears.

WHAT SHE DOES FOR ME:

1. makes me feel free
2. feels me freak maze
3. takes me far away
4. she loves me (she does anything I say)
5. spills her magic spermcount into some stranger's amorous transgression
6. allows me to abandon myself and seek out eternal bliss
7. neutralizes the foreign agent series and postejaculates Big Love

8. forces me to create an untenable survival mode that blemishes my record
9. instigates my drifting into the borderless beyond where my ART fucks all
10. covers me like a suicidal glove now departing out of gate 10

This makes for a wholesome entre

This makes for a wholesome entrepreneur

This makes for a wholesome enterprise. Time watch campaign promises to laugh indiscriminate lunar module in fellatio mode. Smile smokes intact while foreign bloodhounds transmit AIDS relocation plan. Continental schematics break fast and head for the long sought after goal posts of artificial intelligence. Culture Czar rams kiddy car into cattycorner & old man with pea knuckles skimming the rim of her ass folds his hand and vanishes. All of a sudden The Tofu Toughs come into town and The Soybean Revolution is underway. Birkenstock sandals trounce the pavement as designer walking sticks smash through the plate glass of all local establishments. Tears stream down the faces of entrepreneurial hustlers as they watch their bucks flee the country unharmed and ready for action. Third World glut manifests itself absolutely no destiny at all while Gore-Tex rivalry resonates stopwatch sentimentality. Aint over till it's over. Fortified with vitamin lewd.

Kaleidoscopic karma kandy eyes send shivers down my

skeleton as it skanks to a reggae beat. Chocolate hazelnut coffee turns coal miner's daughter into early morning combustion engine. She readies herself for the next serial murder. News transmission traverses her other body eruption. Touching base and reintegrating the plural persona back into his pink and purplish pulp. The pansy daisy hibiscus rose hips shaking radiant raindance while hair monster enterprise schemes more gaseous realities. Science sinks into selfsolace practice of nowhere else to go while aesthetic hustler hypes new improved way to interpret the death of millenia. Meet The Regime. They're comfy and cute. Bottled up and ready to blow.

Daily drudge activities sensitizes ego's plan to detract from system build-up while welfare mothers coalesce supreme vindication of sexdrive forces. Stripping veil of confusion revealing a face-the-facts mortality and divine recognition (she transplants her hundred baby episode into the suicide tent at the fair). What's fair is fair and what's not gets caught. Guns melting hickory butter on a flesh of toast. The mood is tranquil as TV products scream for her attention. Rose Hips persuades the governing party to reconsider. For lunch: more sound bites.

seemingly static status quo lawncare creates glut of moonscape powerwalk control devices narrate false disposition of polltakers unable to commit themselves to chaos deprivation sleaze campaign sensationalizes stupor of ethics panel inquiry wilding forces turn Park-N-Ride subplot into grave consequences fictional rhythm persuades the Institution to keep on

going advantageous ads lead corruptible mass into
new headtrip service sector vectors and vipers turn
into lawless mentors and soulless snipers the view
from up here is great better late than never
having your fifteen minutes of social occasion

blankFrank ambiance struggling to
record the desire of difference
in open market assignment.

Periodic fundamentalist hype regime
creams bacteria mode sexual
interlude consummates rubber testing.

Sperm explodes through gelatinous haiku
as words withdraw into
ancient armpit of memory.

The Odor of Things To Come.

Resting in the bowel movement of
the new Silent Majority there comes
a time to strangulate the artist's impudence.

Car   commercials   sell   off   neutralized   gun
   control   laws   as   stress   factors   penetrate
     the   insatiable   mind.

Hoodwinks   surgically   alter   the   hypothalmus   and
rain   forest   depletion   enables   ersatz   meat   control
agents   to   denigrate   next   expressionist   project.

Mass   transit   churchstop   and   pitted   ego   mechanics
   alter   boygirl   ratio   while   monkeylust   sovereignty
     screams.

Freeing the zookeeper while maintaining the value of clit.

Skin melts blue germ warfare   as biomorphic insecticide
does harmonious fratricide   while bumping rear genders

Language crunch with homogenous milk
mixed with organic brown rice syrup
streamlines a mainstream cause and defect syndrome. All
overwrought and sometimes bought-out plutocracies renege
on deals cut two decades ago.

IV. Post-World Fundamentalism: Baudrillard and MTV

face it: the facts disintegrate yet perpetuate perverse acts of violence in the name of war (drugs, sex, oil, art, pleasure with a purpose). then you try to figure it out & before you can make heads or tails over it gaseous fumes pervade the scene you struggle to subsist in and the world never seems the same again. start over?

displace it: the inner turmoil manifesting the changes taking place within your eroticized psyche-self forces you to reconsider everything you've ever done with your life. you're a three-dimensional nothing-nobody traversing the edge of The Fourth Dimension and everything seems to be getting way out of control. there's no one left to insist that you do things certain ways (only Institutions are willing to do that) so now it's up to you to provide your itinerant psyche-self with all these pleasure-trip options meanwhile all you can do is slobber over the patent leather boot of the idiot robot with golden handcuffs snapped against his wrists. this is called "getting off". this is called "arrested emotional development" with pseudo-self-confidence pseudo-self-control no "self" to speak of. this is called Love Amerikan Style. you're totally fucking useless and unless you start becoming more productive (less eroticized, less inclined to pursue the ultimate in pleasure-tripping) no one will want to speak to you. you're enslaved by media props bopping their subliminal totalitarian substance all over your head (the slimy substance molds whatever persona you might think you have developing for you : it's by far THE LATEST FASHION). feel the heat?

trace it: mark your words as they come from your intransigent psyche-self (hypereroticized) and see the gaseous eros flow out in nonsequiters guaranteeing you the right to be whoever the fuck you want to be and then if possible send check or money order to me at Identity / P.O. Box 241 / Boulder CO / 80306. either start the rampant fucking and get off on it or else be fucked and then die of nothing exceptional except your own stupidity and lack of perseverance. you're doing nothing so nothing has a way of making you do more of the same (nothing). this leads to epidemic disgust with your psyche-self (de-eroticized). eventually you'll be unable to recover from the horrid stench of burning flesh and everything you say and do will be a direct result of the violent acts being perpetrated by the perverts who run your dreams. your dreams are shit multiplied to the nth degree. have an orgy?

face it: the facts regurgitate and the garbage barge barges in on your video complacent mind so that now you feel you have to deal with it. the mind is a terrible thing to waste so please by all means be sure to send that check or money order **right now!** to Identity / P.O. Box 241 / Boulder CO / 80306. the frazzled frenzied frankenchrist that crawls inside your body is stalking the psyche-self in hopes of obliterating whatever desire may be floating within you. a big idiot with catastrophic eyes pinning down any potential escape route frankenchrist is now emerging in your shit. transplanting shit for brains and waste for psyche-self enables him to control your dreams. this is where we're at right now. is there any way out? if only we could start a band and change the world. wouldn't *that* be fun?

INTRODUCING THE BLACK ICE BOOKS SERIES:

The Black Ice Books Series will introduce readers to the new generation of dissident writers in revolt. Breaking out of the age-old traditions of mainstream literature, the voices published here are at once ribald, caustic, controversial, and inspirational. These books signal a reflowering of the art underground. They explore iconoclastic styles that celebrate life vis-à-vis the spirit of their unrelenting energy and anger. Similar to the recent explosion in the alternative music scene, these books point toward a new counterculture rage that's just now finding its way into the mainstream discourse. The Black Ice Books Series brings to readers the most radical fiction being written in America today.

The Kafka Chronicles
A novel by Mark Amerika
The Kafka Chronicles investigates the world of passionate sexual experience while simultaneously ridiculing everything that is false and primitive in our contemporary political discourse. Mark Amerika's first novel ignites hyper-language that explores the relationship between style and substance, self and sexuality, and identity and difference. His energetic prose uses all available tracks, mixes vocabularies, and samples genres. Taking its cue from the recent explosion of angst-driven rage found in the alternative rock music scene, this book reveals the unsettled voice of America's next generation.

Mark Amerika has lived in Florida, New York, California, and different parts of Europe, and has worked as a free-lance bicycle courier, lifeguard, video cameraman, and greyhound racing official. Amerika's fiction has appeared in many magazines, including *Fiction International*, *Witness*, the German publication *Lettre International*, and *Black Ice*, of which he is editor. He is presently writing a "violent concerto for deconstructive guitar" in Boulder, Colorado.

"Mark Amerika not only plays music—the rhythm, the sound of his words and sentences—he plays verbal meanings as if they're music. I'm not just talking about music. Amerika is showing us that William Burroughs came out of jazz knowledge and that now everything's political—and everything's coming out through the lens of sexuality…"

—Kathy Acker

Paper, ISBN: 0-932511-54-6, $7.00

Revelation Countdown
Short Fiction by Cris Mazza

While in many ways reaffirming the mythic dimension of being on the road already romaticized in American pop and folk culture, *Revelation Countdown* also subtly undermines that view. These stories project onto the open road not the nirvana of personal freedom but rather a type of freedom more closely resembling loss of control. Being in constant motion and passing through new environments destabilizes life, casts it out of phase, heightens perception, skews reactions. Every little problem is magnified to overwhelming dimensions; events segue from slow motion to fast forward; background noises intrude, causing perpetual wee-hour insomnia. In such an atmosphere, the title *Revelation Countdown*, borrowed from a roadside sign in Tennessee, proves prophetic: It may not arrive at 7:30, but revelation will inevitably find the traveler.

Cris Mazza is the author of two previous collections of short fiction, *Animal Acts* and *Is It Sexual Harassment Yet?* and a novel, *How to Leave a Country.* She has resided in Brooklyn, New York; Clarksville, Tennessee; and Meadville, Pennsylvania; but she has always lived in San Diego, California.

"...fictions that are remarkable for the force and freedom of their imaginative style."

—*New York Times Book Review*

Paper, ISBN: 0-932511-73-2, $7.00

Avant-Pop: Fiction for a Daydream Nation
Edited by Larry McCaffery

In *Avant-Pop*, Larry McCaffery has assembled a collection of innovative fiction, comic book art, illustrations, and other unclassifiable texts written by the most radical, subversive, literary talents of the postmodern new wave. The authors included here vary in background, from those with well-established reputations as cult figures in the pop underground (Samuel R. Delany, Kathy Acker, Ferret, Derek Pell, Harold Jaffe), and important new figures who have gained prominence since the late eighties (Mark Leyner, Eurudice, William T. Vollmann), to, finally, the most promising new kids on the block.

Avant-Pop is meant to send a collective wake-up call to all those readers who spent the last decade nodding off, along with the rest of America's daydream nation. To those readers and critics who have decried the absence of genuinely radicalized art capable of liberating people from the bland roles and assumptions they've accepted in our B-movie society of the spectacle, *Avant-Pop* announces that reports about the death of a literary avant-garde have been greatly exaggerated.

Larry McCaffery's most recent books include *Storming the Reality Studio: A Casebook of Cyberpunk and Postmodern SF* and *Across the Wounded Galaxies: Interviews with Contemporary American SF Writers*.
Paper, ISBN: 0-932511-72-4, $7.00

New Noir
Stories by John Shirley
In *New Noir*, John Shirley, like a postmodern Edgar Allen Poe, depicts minds deformed into fantastic configurations by the pressure, the very weight, of an entire society bearing down on them. "Jody and Annie on TV," selected by the editor of *Mystery Scene* as "perhaps the most important story...in years in the crime fiction genre," reflects the fact that whole segments of zeitgeist and personal psychology have been supplanted by the mass media, that the average kid on the streets in Los Angeles is in a radical crisis of exploded self-image, and that life really is meaningless for millions. The stories here also bring to mind Elmore Leonard and the better crime novelists, but John Shirley—unlike writers who attempt to extrapolate from peripheral observation and research—bases his stories on his personal experience of extreme people and extreme mental states, and his struggle with the seductions of drugs, crime, prostitution, and violence.

John Shirley was born in Houston, Texas in 1953 but spent the majority of his youth in Oregon. He has been a lead singer in a rock band, Obsession, writes lyrics for various bands, including Blue Oyster Cult, and in his spare time records with the Panther Moderns. He is the author of numerous works in a variety of genres; his story collection *Heatseeker* was chosen by the Locus Reader's Poll as one of the best collections of 1989. His latest novel is *Wetbones*.

"John Shirley serves up the bloody heart of a rotting society with the aplomb of an Aztec surgeon on Dexedrine."

—ALA Booklist

Paper, ISBN: 0-932511-55-4, $7.00

Individuals may order any or all of the Black Ice Book series directly from Fiction Collective Two, 4950/Publication Unit, Illinois State University, Normal, IL 61761. (Check or money order only, made payable to Fiction Collective Two.) Bookstore, library, and text orders should be placed through the distributor: The Talman Company, Inc., 131 Spring Street, #201 E-N, New York, NY 10012; Customer Service: 800/537-8894.